WILD BLOOD

Also by A.C. Abbott

Branded

WILD BLOOD

A.C. ABBOTT

CUTTING EDGE

ISBN-13: 978-1-952138-91-1

Published by
Cutting Edge Books
PO Box 8212
Calabasas, CA 91372
www.cuttingedgebooks.com

CHAPTER ONE

A s HIS sorrel horse plunged out of the dusty wagon road, Jim Dixon dove headlong out of the saddle, swearing with startled fervency. He lit on his left shoulder and rolled swiftly under the sheltering branches of a gnarled old mesquite, his Colt .45 coming smoothly out of his holster into his big hand. Back in the dust of the road lay his wide-brimmed black hat, two small round holes marking the path of a bullet through its crown.

That rifle slug, tearing through the drowsy afternoon without warning, had coldly checked Jim's mounting eagerness to see the old home ranch again. Now he lay quiet, a big black-headed man of twenty-five, with an unyielding glint in his iron-gray eyes.

"Hell of a welcome," he grunted belligerently, then added with grim reflection, "but I should have known. Grant Talbot isn't a man to forget—or forgive."

Absolute silence fell over the brush-studded flat. Jim's glance probed narrowly at the tangle of mesquite and catclaw bordering a dry wash a hundred yards farther up the road, but he saw nothing. Cautiously he twisted around for a look at his horses.

Cappy, the big chestnut sorrel he had been riding, had stopped in the open fifteen feet away, while the dun pack horse had pulled up just beyond. Both horses stood with heads thrown high, their ears pointing like accusing fingers at a spot considerably above where the road crossed the wash.

"Up that way, huh?"

Jim twisted back, squirming forward so that he could see past the knotty trunk of the old tree. As he did so, he heard a sudden cracking of brush, then the swift, rhythmic drum of a running horse. The sound faded rapidly away toward the town of Pinal, five miles distant.

For a moment Jim lay rigid, puzzled and wary. It didn't seem logical that anyone who wanted to kill him would pull out of a fight in which he was pinned down, six-gun against rifle, but another glance at his horses convinced him that such was the case. Both animals had lowered their heads in search of tender green shoots of spring grass.

Abruptly Jim crawled out from under the thorny branches and stood up, holstering his gun and scowling darkly at the thin streamer of dust that marked the retreat of his unknown assailant.

"He shore changed his mind in a hurry," he muttered in wonder. "Now, what the hell was the idea of that little reception committee?"

He continued to scowl as he absently brushed dust from his gray flannel shirt and hitched up his worn batwing chaps. He retrieved his hat, staring at the holes in the crown without really seeing them. A dull disappointment nagged at him and a hope, only half formed, was struggling to stay alive.

He had been running wild horses in northern California when he got his dad's message, and he had sold his outfit and started south at once. Old Long John Dixon, not knowing Jim's address, had written to a mutual friend, saying merely, "Tell Jim to come home." The very starkness of the request carried a warning, but Jim had still dared to hope that the killing of Dick Talbot had been forgotten.

"That wasn't Grant," he mused, glancing again at the receding spiral of dust, "or he'd never have pulled out. But I'll still bet it was one of his Ladder cowboys. Hell!" He broke off sharply. "*She'd* never forget, anyway."

Thought of the fair-haired, blue-eyed sister of Dick and Grant Talbot drove Jim to abrupt, swift action. Swinging onto Capp's back, he spurred the horse into a lope toward the dry wash and turned into it, searching for the place where the bushwhacker had lain in wait.

He soon found it, a spot where the bank was high enough to conceal a horse. The sandy bed of the wash was littered with cigarette stubs, indicating that the man had waited for some time. Jim could not locate the cartridge casing, but he did find something else that interested him greatly.

On the dead, broken limb of a stunted mesquite hung a scrap of gray checkered cloth. Jim remembered the sudden cracking of brush and knew beyond a doubt that this piece of cloth had been snagged out of the drygulcher's shirt. With almost reverent care he pulled it loose and fondled it in his big brown hand while a slow grin stretched his lips.

"Our little playmate," he informed Cappy with dry humor, "got in too big a hurry. When I find the rest of this shirt, I'll know who was so doggone glad to see me and—God! I hope he's not wearin' a Ladder brand!"

He stowed the scrap of cloth in his shirt pocket and rolled a quick cigarette before reining out of the wash and heading once more toward town, the pack horse plodding along behind like a bored shadow. Across the valley to the northeast, beyond the town of Pinal, Jim could see the familiar deep notch in the jagged Pinal Mountains, below which lay Five Drag in a beautiful, well-watered canyon. Barring further encounters with hidden riflemen, he would be there before the sun disappeared over the Caballo del Muerto Mountains behind him.

The mesquites thinned, giving way to more open country over which soapweeds towered like ragged sentinels. The valley was starting to green up as a result of spring rains, but it showed plainly the ravages of dry hard years in the recent past. Nevertheless, Jim found this desert land, for all its harshness, more exhilarating than all the lush northern sections he had visited during the past four years. This was home range.

As he rode, his glance kept swiveling up the center of the wide basin toward the spot where the Ladder headquarters lay hidden in a clump of cottonwoods. He couldn't see the spread; but he could see altogether too clearly in his mind a lithe slender form that was usually clad in Levis and boots, a sweet oval face warmed by the sun to a rich golden tan. He could see red smiling lips, and he could feel the touch of those lips . . . .

"Hell!" he burst out with sudden savagery. "She's probably married. Four years is a long time."

Telling himself this, however, didn't keep his eyes from flicking toward the north every few minutes, and thus it was that he saw a wisp of dust coming down the Ladder trail toward its junction with the Pinal road. That trail, he remembered, came in at the bottom of a brushy draw where natural barriers and erosion had created a good dirt tank for the storage of rain water.

Jim did not increase his pace, since he didn't care to stir up much dust himself, but he did pull his .30-30 from its scabbard under his leg. He levered a shell into the barrel and rested the gun across the saddle in front of him, wondering with narrow speculation whether that rider was the man who had welcomed him so warmly.

As he rode down into the draw, he saw that the water hole was dry, its basin caked and rutted from the hoofs of hundreds of cattle. The spring rains had been sufficient to start the grass, but it would take the heavy rains of summer to replenish such scattered water holes as this.

He could hear the faint thud of a galloping horse now, and he pulled out of the road, making a short circle through heavy brush that carried him below the junction of the Ladder trail. Here he pulled up, behind a stand of mesquite thick enough to conceal his horses except from the wariest eye, and waited. The realization that the rider might be Grant Talbot himself shortened Jim's breath and narrowed his eyes but did not weaken his resolve to get a look at him. He just might be wearing a gray checkered shirt.

The rider came on steadily. As he rounded the trail into the road, Jim caught a brief glimpse of a bay horse but could not see who was riding him. Then, when the bay was nearly abreast, Jim jumped Cappy out into the road, his rifle ominously ready.

The bay shied violently, nearly throwing his rider, who pulled him to a rearing halt. It was not until the horse came down with a wild snort that Jim got a good look at the person on him. Marilyn Talbot!

Shock held him momentarily rigid, staring at her while four years' worth of dreams faded before reality. Her brown Stetson was pulled low, but it could not conceal the deep, expressive blue eyes, nor could it contain the fair, almost silvery hair that curled softly around her cheeks. Her startled expression gave way suddenly to stunned recognition, and she caught her breath sharply.

"Jim!"

"Marilyn, I—"

Not until he reached for his hat did he realize that he still held his rifle, pointing directly at her. Hastily he rammed it into the scabbard and pulled the hat from his head, struggling with a riot in his chest that threatened to choke him. Somehow he managed to keep his voice level and characteristically cool.

"Shore didn't expect to bump into you so quick. How are you?"

Her eyes flashed over him, lingering for a moment on the holstered gun at his thigh before coming back to his face, searchingly. Those eyes were a deeper blue than Jim remembered, like bottomless lakes at sunset, a change that must have been caused by grief and worry.

Jim felt his face grow tight under their critical scrutiny. He replaced his hat, tilted back, and rolled a cigarette, waiting for her to speak.

"I—heard you were coming back," she said finally with an effort.

"Yeah," he agreed dryly, "I figured somebody knew it. Got my forty-dollar bonnet perforated already."

As he lit his cigarette, he bent his head so she could see the bullet holes. Then he straightened, inhaling deeply and gazing at her through the smoke.

She was eying him uncertainly, her full lower lip caught between her teeth in a nervous gesture he well remembered. "Who took that shot at you?"

He shrugged. "He left his callin card, but he forgot to put his brand on it." With apparent indifference he pulled the scrap of cloth from his pocket and held it out. "Know anybody wears a shirt like this?"

She gave the cloth only a quick glance and nodded guardedly. "Several people around here. Judge Miller got in a whole box of those shirts a while back, and the boys liked them."

"Uh-huh. Well, *one* of the boys needs a patchin' job."

"And you're thinking it was one of the Ladder boys?"

Jim eyed her steadily as he returned the cloth to his pocket. "I was hopin' it wasn't," he said significantly.

"But you were still lying in wait here," she said with heat, as if that proved him a liar.

"Shore. I saw your dust comin' and didn't know who was under it. That jigger can't shoot too straight, but he might do a better job if he was behind me."

Her eyes held him for a moment before flicking beyond him. Her nether lip was once more caught between her white even teeth and her breathing seemed hampered, her breasts rising and falling with a quick rhythm. She seemed unaware that the horses, striking up an acquaintance, had brought them very close together; but her nearness kindled a long smoldering fire in Jim's blood.

Covertly he stole a glance at her left hand as it rested on the saddle horn. Ringless! Jim's heart bounded, but he held his wild exultation in check. That might not mean a thing. Still, most ranch girls were married at twenty-two unless they had been thwarted by a love affair they couldn't forget.

The meager hope Jim had cherished was springing to glorious life until she looked at him again. Evidently whatever confusion she had felt at this meeting had been overcome and her eyes had grown coolly hostile, shoving him away.

"Why did you come back after all this time?" she demanded.

"Dad sent for me."

"Why?"

"He didn't say," Jim retorted, nettled. He could feel her drawing farther and farther away from him, and he was powerless to stop it. "Just said for me to come home."

"I can tell you why," she said with a hard evenness. "He's going broke and—"

"Broke? How come?"

"We've had three terribly dry years and there's been—other trouble." She hesitated and then went on that same impersonal voice. "He probably thinks you can straighten things out, but you can't. You'll only make them worse."

Her attitude, almost brutal, it seemed to Jim, stung him to coldness. "I'm not looking for trouble."

"You're carrying a rifle."

"You're damn right I'm carrying a rifle, and I'll use it on anybody who tries to use one on me!"

"Then you are looking for trouble!"

Jim pulled in a deep breath, clamping down on his anger. "I was hopin'," he said deliberately, "that Dad sent for me because the trouble was over, but I should have known better."

"That kind of trouble," she said bitterly, "doesn't get over."

Jim took a deep drag from his cigarette and looked away, far over the scraggly brush to the mountains looming black in the distance. He had known, for four long, lonely years, that she would never forgive him, but a tiny spark of hope had kept burning in his heart. It wasn't fair, and he wondered, as he had wondered so many times during those four years, if she had any way of knowing that it wasn't.

"How are your folks?" he asked gruffly.

"Mother's all right. Dad died three years ago."

"Grant runnin' the outfit now?"

"Certainly."

A thought, as swift and sure as lightning, flashed into Jim's mind: The fact that Grant Talbot was now running Ladder undoubtedly accounted for some of the other trouble in the valley. Old Man Talbot, tall and straight, with the light hair and blue eyes that marked all three of his children, was as fair and honest a man as Jim ever hoped to meet; but the blood of his first wife, the mother of Grant and Dick, must have been curdled.

"I'm sorry about your dad," he said presently. "He was as square as they come."

"Yes, he was. He—failed in health right after Dick was killed, and never got over it."

Again Jim felt his skin grow tight but he faced her squarely. "Marilyn, did you ever hear how that happened?"

"Certainly. Grant told me."

"Did he tell you the truth?"

"Do you think he'd lie to me?" she snapped hotly.

"I'm not sayin' he would, but what did he tell you?"

"That you got drunk and started rubbing it into Dick about a maverick you'd stolen from him. That you rode him with spurs, razzed him until he finally couldn't stand it any longer and reached for his gun."

Jim turned cold all over. Her steady gaze, inscrutable and yet challenging, seemed to go clear through him.

"If you believe that," he said tightly, "you won't believe me, but I'll tell you anyway."

"Save your breath," she said shortly, and started to rein past him.

A knot exploded in Jim's breast and he jumped Cappy forward, dropping his cigarette and grabbing Marilyn's wrist in a steel grip that made her wince.

"I'll talk and you'll listen," he said in hard accents. "Dave, Judge Miller, Old Brady will back me up. Everybody at the roundup except your brothers agreed that maverick was mine. The boys picked him up high on the mountain above the ranch, so I branded him. That night *Dick* got drunk and started calling me names."

He paused, hating to tell her the truth about the no-good brother she had loved blindly, but driven by her defiant glare.

"I didn't want to fight him, Marilyn. I tried to reason with him at first. When I saw he was too mean drunk to listen, I started to walk out. He shot me—in the back! I was down. I had to kill him—or let him kill me!"

"I heard that version," she said coldly. "I didn't believe it."

"It's true, so help me God! Do you think I wanted to kill your brother, knowin' how you felt about him?"

"If it was self-defense, why did you run away?"

"Because I knew if I stuck around I'd have to tangle with Grant, and I figured I'd already hurt you bad enough."

"You left on my account?"

"Why else? Did you think I was afraid of that—"

Jim snapped his teeth against his scathing opinion of Grant Talbot. For a moment Marilyn seemed to hestitate, searching his face. Then she jerked her wrist away, and her voice trembled with suppressed bitterness.

"If you were so madly in love with me, why didn't you ever write?"

"I wanted to," he said desperately. "I wanted to come see you before I left, but I—didn't figure you'd want to see me. All I could think of was you, Marilyn. You didn't know Dick like—"

"He was wild," she interrupted, her eyes flaring with challenge, "but he was just a kid."

"He was a year older than I was!"

"Yes," she said, dropping into an acrid, calculating drawl, "you were just a kid then, too, but I hear you've been practicing since. Dick was just the first man you killed!"

Jim cut off the idea with a savage gesture, but he couldn't penetrate the hard front she'd built up.

"It sounds very noble to say that you left on my account, but knowing that I feel the same way about Grant didn't keep you from coming back, did it?"

"I told you Dad sent for me."

"Of course, but did you expect me to welcome you with open arms? I've only got one brother left, you know, and I love him too."

"Love him?" Jim said hotly. "After the way he lied to you?"

She looked him over with measured scorn before saying deliberately, "I still don't think he's the one who's lying."

That hurt, worse than if she'd slapped him. He said harshly, "And I had the damn-fool idea you were in love with me."

"I was, once, but I got over it, the same as you did."

Jim fought down an almost irresistible desire to grab her and show her how he'd got over it, but pride held him quiet.

"It took quite a while," she admitted, as if ashamed of her weakness, "but when Grant told me about the gun fights you've had since you left here—"

"Grant, huh? Your darlin' brother didn't pass up any chance to put me in wrong, did he?"

"Grant," she said, "was thinking of my happiness."

"Huh!" Jim rolled and lit a cigarette. Then he straightened in the saddle, pulled his hat down low, and eyed her coolly from the shadow of the brim. "Marilyn, it's shore been nice seein' you again," he drawled with mild irony. "I was kinda hopin,' when I first hit the valley, that I wouldn't have to renew acquaintances with Grant, but now—" He shrugged as he lifted the reins. "If you love the skunk, you better tell him to lay off me."

He nodded briefly, pulled Cappy around, and, driving the pack horse in front of him, spurred toward town.

CHAPTER TWO

Jim pulled to a walk at the mouth of the long lane leading past Judge Miller's ranch into the main street of the village. His hands were clammy with sweat in spite of the cold lump that lay inside him. He had told himself repeatedly that Marilyn must despise him, but actually hearing it from her lips left him with a dull, empty feeling.

At the same time he was made restless by vague, fleeting doubts. Why had she asked him why he'd never written? Was it possible that she had wanted to believe he was not to blame, that she had needed only reassurance of his love to forgive him and take him back?

The thought made Jim writhe, and he swore viciously. If there ever had been such a time, it was undoubtedly gone now, and regretful speculation could only torture him. Ruthlessly he shoved it out of his mind, turning his attention to his surroundings.

They didn't have a cheering effect. Even the Judge's place, always an oasis in this desert valley, showed the strain of the past three years. The old cottonwoods along the creek bottom were as green as ever, but the fields of hay and grain beyond were brown with drought. The sprawling orchards of peach and apple, which had always been carpeted by a thick matting of green grass, now rose out of a jungle of weeds.

At first glance the town itself showed very few changes. The stage station still sat pompously at the junction of this road with the one that ran from Devil's Pass on north to Fort Irby. As he reined south onto this main street, his eye rested on many familiar signs and buildings: Judge Miller's general store, the hotel, and, across the street to the east, the Mescal saloon. Farther along, down next to the creek, were the scattered corrals of the stage livery. At this hour of the afternoon the town appeared lazy and practically deserted, with only a few saddle horses lining the street.

The tingle of pleasure Jim had expected to feel on riding back to Pinal was sadly lacking. He thought briefly of a number of old friends that he had intended to look up as soon as he hit town. Now, however, he decided to get a quick beer and a sack of tobacco at the Mescal and ride on out to Five Drag.

As he started past Miller's store, a cowboy stepped out onto the awninged boardwalk, his rolled-brim hat shoved carelessly back on his curly brown head, a cigarette dangling from his thin lips. He tipped one shoulder against a porch post and regarded Jim through squinted brown eyes.

"Who left the gate open?" he inquired mildly.

Jim swung over to the rail and stepped to the ground, his grin of pleasure held somewhat in check by a grudging uncertainty. He and Eddie Worthington had, on more than one occasion, raised enough hell together to last the whole country for a week; but that had been before the fateful night when Dick Talbot went down.

Now Jim couldn't be sure where he stood with this old friend. He ducked under the rail without taking his eyes off the cowboy and mounted the porch to extend his hand.

"Howdy, Eddie. How you doin'?"

"Can't complain." Eddie's grin was lazy, but his eyes were sparking with a reckless light that Jim well remembered. His handshake was heartily warming. "Heard you were headin' back this way, Jim. You're shore lookin' prosperous."

"I've been eatin' regular," Jim admitted.

He reached for tobacco, letting his glance range down over the lithe figure of the cowboy, noting with unchanging expression that Eddie now wore a second gun, low and tied down on his left side.

Jim touched a match to his cigarette and asked casually "You still workin' for Ladder?"

"Hell, no." Eddie spat disgustedly. "Not for over two years now."

Jim pulled in a deep breath and let it out in a happy laugh, clapping a glad hand on his friend's shoulder. "Doggone, it's good to see you again, cowboy. What you doin' these days?"

"Tryin' to stay out of trouble, mostly," Eddie replied with a grin. "That's a full-time job around here these days."

"Yeah, I—"

At that moment Jim's eye alighted on a familiar figure emerging from the hotel a few doors down the street, and a cold thrill shot through him, followed instantly by the leap of flaming hatred. How well he remembered the tall lithe figure, the wide shoulders, the swaggering walk! Grant Talbot had always hit him like a hard fist right in the eye, and now the feeling was magnified a hundredfold.

Talbot was dressed like any working cowboy, spurred boots, leather chaps, heavy blue shirt, and the inevitable belted gun. Jim's eye lingered a moment on that gun, swinging low on the right side with the butt flaring out as if awaiting a ready hand.

A slight, wiry cowboy stepped out behind Talbot, and the two men turned up the street without hesitation, their spurs clanking heavily. There was no doubt that they had seen Jim from the hotel lobby. He recognized the cowboy as a man named Rennick who had been a very close friend of Dick Talbot's. And Rennick was wearing a gray checkered shirt.

At the sound of the thudding boots, Eddie glanced up at Jim sharply. Then, without looking behind him, he tossed his cigarette away and turned with an indolence Jim knew was faked. He didn't turn completely around, but leaned back with the post between his shoulder blades, lifting one spurred boot to the post and hooking his right thumb in his cartridge belt. He displayed only a mild curiosity.

Deliberately Jim stepped away from Eddie and swung to face the approaching men, momentarily chilled by a painful memory. He had seen another Talbot striding toward him with this same arrogant carriage, the same stony expression made merciless by narrowed, glittering eyes. He had labored under a terrible restraint that night, thinking of Marilyn.

Thought of her now, however, only augmented his reckless, driving enmity toward this man who had ruined what chance might have been left to him. And when he saw the jagged hole in the left sleeve of Rennick's shirt, the last vestige of restraint dropped from him. He took a last drag from his cigarette and flipped it away, resting his hands on his hips and waiting with an insolent nonchalance.

As Talbot came to a stop five feet away, Rennick stepped past him and a little to one side so that he faced Eddie across the square. It was a significant move that told Jim even more about Eddie's present stature than had the second gun.

Talbot allowed an insulting gaze to range down over Jim's figure. "I heard you were coming back," he said.

Jim's answer was blunt. "That's no news to me."

"I ran you out of this country once, Dixon," Talbot went on, ignoring Jim's remark, "and I'll do it again."

"I don't remember that you had anything to do with my leavin'," Jim drawled coolly. "Shore I've got no memory, but you wouldn't think a feller'd forget a thing like that."

"You'd better not forget it again!"

"Why, hell," Jim murmured pleasantly. "I got the idea this afternoon that you wanted me to stay here, permanent. Or was Rennick just supposed to do a little scoutin' and come right home?"

Talbot's eyes narrowed dangerously. "Just what do you mean by that?"

With taunting indifference Jim slid his glance over to Rennick, meeting the cowboy's defiant eyes for a moment before looking directly at his torn sleeve. As indifferently as he had made his inspection, he lifted his left hand to his shirt pocket and pulled out the scrap of cloth, extending it carelessly.

His voice, however, had gone hard. "I reckon you'll need this when you get ready to do your mendin'."

Rennick flashed a quick, startled look at the cloth, then took a slow step backward, his right arm hooking as his eyes shuttled uncertainly between Jim and Eddie. Jim was aware that Eddie hadn't moved, but Talbot's hands were free at his sides, the right one splayed and ready.

Jim's own right hand was quivering, his breath shallow and tight as he waited. He saw the decision come into Rennick's eyes; but before it could be carried out, a horse flashed around the corner and a feminine scream shot an icy bolt through Jim's nerves.

"Don't!"

After that one convulsive shiver, Jim turned as rigid as stone. He saw Rennick give up his purpose with obvious relief, and Jim shifted his piercing eyes fully to Grant, who was still ready to fight. Then Marilyn was among them, her hat gone, her fair hair flying wildly as she flung herself at Grant.

"Grant, don't! For God's sake, don't! He'll kill you!"

For a strained instant Grant's glittering gaze held on Jim over Marilyn's shoulder. Then he turned those glittering eyes down to her and spoke through stiff lips. "Don't ever do that again."

With a wrench, he jerked away from her and wheeled out into the street, striding toward his horse with fury showing in very taut muscle. Rennick was right behind him, trotting to keep up.

Marilyn stood rooted, watching them until they had vaulted into their saddles and whirled out of town. Then she spun violently to glare at Eddie, her little fists doubled at her sides. He still hadn't moved, nor did he now, meeting her fiery gaze with a somber steadiness that held neither defiance nor apology.

Jim, slowly easing out of his tension, saw that look, and it checked him, bringing him up hard against a disturbing thought. He was still staring at Eddie, wondering, when Marilyn turned on him.

"You bloodthirsty devil!" she gritted through clenched teeth.

Her eyes swept over him like a hot wind. Then she turned her back on him, flung herself into the saddle, and galloped out of town without looking at either of them again.

Jim, staring after her until she had disappeared, suddenly ducked his head and fumbled for tobacco. His face was flaming, his heart hammering under the realization of what he had done. Far from avoiding a fight with the only brother she had left, he had deliberately tried to bait him into one, and would have succeeded except for her intervention.

If she had ever wanted to believe that he used a gun unwillingly, she wouldn't believe it now. And he still cared . . . .

"Light?"

Jim looked up, startled, to find that Eddie was holding a match for him. Hastily he accepted the light, shamed into self-control by the fact that his hands were trembling.

"Thanks," he murmured, then lifted a squinted gaze to his friend and grinned. "From the way Rennick was sidlin' away from you, I take it you been buildin' yourself a rep."

"You got no room to talk, cowboy. From what *I* hear, I'm wonderin' if there's any men left aboveground up in Montana."

"A few," Jim conceded, his grin broadening with embarrassment. "How in the devil did you all get wind of that?"

Eddie laughed but had no chance to answer. A heavy hand on Jim's shoulder spun him around to face a big, heavy-set man whose hair showed gray around the temples, whose eyes squinted keenly out of a leathery face, and whose worn black vest supported the tarnished badge of a deputy sheriff.

"You're under arrest," he said evenly, "for disturbin' the peace, packin' a gun in public, talkin' to Eddie Worthington, and just plain bein' too damned easy to look at."

"Is that all?" Jim blurted in consternation.

"That's all for now, but from the way you're startin' out, I'll have you up for mayhem d'rectly."

Jim laughed as he extended his hand. "Skeet, how are you?"

"A little better, thanks." Skeet Dorman returned both the handshake and the grin, which wrinkled his face until his eyes were nearly closed.

"You're a long ways from that easy chair, aren't you?" Jim asked jokingly. "As I remember, nothin' short of a massacre could get you away from those saloons over in Wilson."

"Country won't let a man drink in peace any more."

"How so?"

"Aw, hell!" Dorman stepped to the edge of the walk to spit disgustedly. "Everybody says everybody else is stealin' from them; stages bein' robbed faster'n they can collect the silver to get stole; men dyin' off so sudden they can't tell you what ailed 'em."

"What ailed 'em? Or who?" Eddie put in.

"Well—" Dorman grinned. "It's no secret *what* ailed 'em."

"Sounds like the country's really pickin' up," Jim said dryly.

"Yeah," Dorman agreed, giving Jim a hard, level glance, "and you want to keep your eyes peeled or we'll be pickin' you up. That man Rennick don't follow the rules of civilized warfare."

"I found that out," Jim acknowledged, "but it don't scare me much. He can't shoot straight enough." He removed his hat to show them the holes in the crown.

"Hell!" Eddie exploded. "There wouldn't have been anything wrong with that shot if you'd had brains enough to fill your hat!"

Jim laughed and dismissed the subject. "Who all's ridin' for Dad now?"

Dorman and Eddie exchanged a quick glance, which filled Jim with apprehension even before Dorman answered softly.

"Dave and old Ramón."

"Is that all?" Jim couldn't conceal the shock that gave him, although he knew from the way both Dorman and Eddie were avoiding his glance that it would do no good to ask questions. He merely said grimly, "He had seven others when I left here."

"Yeah." Dorman sighed wearily. "Well, boys, I gotta hunt up a chunk of shade with a chair in it. You fellers be careful."

"We won't get you up," Eddie assured him with droll good humor.

For several moments after the deputy walked on down the street Jim smoked in silence, prey to a number of dark thoughts. Marilyn had said Five Drag was going broke, and this latest bit of news seemed to back up her statement. Three old men trying to run a spread that ranged over a hundred square miles of territory! Or, Jim thought grimly, that had ranged over that much.

He found himself dreading to face his dad and at the same time restless, eager to talk to him. It seemed like weeks to Jim since he had ridden into the valley, hoping that his trouble with Ladder was a thing of the past, buried with the boy who had started it. Now he was taking it for granted that his dad had sent for him because of trouble with that very outfit.

"You foot-loose?" he asked Eddie suddenly.

Eddie took a deep drag from his cigarette and flipped it into the street before answering. "I'm my own boss, if that's what you mean," he said then.

"How about comin' out to the ranch with me?"

"You mean—take a ridin' job?"

"Yes. I don't know how come Dad's only got two men workin' for him, but I know damn well it's not eough."

"It isn't," Eddie said bluntly, "but are you sure you want me? Some folks say I ain't fit company."

Jim's mind flicked to the second gun Eddie was now wearing, but he kept his eyes glued to the cowboy's face. "I've ridden a lot of trails with you, Eddie," he said evenly. "I never noticed anything wrong with your company."

Eddie's glance wavered and dropped. Very slowly he reached up to pull his hat far down over his face. When he looked up again, there was a queer intense light shining in his eyes.

"Thanks, Jim," he murmured. "I'll think it over."

He lifted one finger in a sort of easygoing salute and turned away, stepping off the walk and heading toward the Mescal without looking back. For a long moment Jim stood immobile, his narrowed gaze fastened on the cowboy's lazily slouching figure. Never before had Eddie shown him such a subtle reserve, and it made him vaguely uneasy.

He recalled the quiet, almost melancholy look that Eddie had given Marilyn, recalled that Marilyn had spun on the cowboy as if shocked at finding him mixed up in that fight. It was all the answer Jim needed. His vaguely uneasy feeling vanished before a quick stab of jealousy and he swung around abruptly, with a muffled curse, and entered the store.

The interior of the long, low building was dim, but Jim didn't hesitate, remembering that the tobacco had always been kept at a counter on the right. As he turned that way, half blinded by the sunlight that was still in his eyes, he ran head on into a girl who had evidently been watching through the open door.

Jim heard her quick gasp and grabbed for her to keep her from falling. Then he quickly stepped back, snatching at his hat.

"Excuse me, ma'am. I—Well, shore it's Donna Miller! Say—" Jim's eyes were becoming accustomed to the gloom now and he used them admiringly, sweeping her slight figure from the top of her dark head to the tips of the slippers showing under her neat blue dress. It was a picture that brought a grin to his face. "You've grown up."

Her dark eyes flashed at him with a hint of resentment. "I wasn't such a kid when you left," she said tartly.

"Only sixteen."

"That's old enough—for 'most anything." Her small round face grew suddenly rosy, lending added warmth to a smile that was as bright as a new day. "Jim, I'm so glad to see you," she said, her voice slightly husky.

She held out her hand and Jim quickly took it, noting how small it was but how well shaped and firm and warm. He had practically forgotten Donna Miller, but now memory of her many inscrutable glances and fiery outbursts in years past filled him with a strange awkwardness.

"Well, Donna, I'm shore glad *somebody's* glad to see me," he said feelingly.

His words brought a fresh crimson wave to her face, and she hastily withdrew her hand. Jim hesitated, puzzled by her seeming inconsistency.

"I need some Durham," he said finally.

As she turned to go behind the counter, his thoughtful gaze followed her. She was not much over five feet tall, but her figure was well rounded and her movements were as light and graceful as the leaves of a tree rippling in the breeze.

He told himself quizzically, You'd have to put a sack of grain on the scales with her to get a readin'.

He replaced his hat, sauntering over to the counter and leaning one elbow on it with comfortable familiarity. "How's your dad?"

"Cranky and lovable as ever." She laughed, but the gay light wouldn't linger in her eyes. They were flitting over his face like nervous swallows. "Jim, you shouldn't have come back," she said with unexpected anxiety. "Oh, it's terribly good to see you again, but it scares me so."

Jim, watching her closely, read something in her expression and her words that startled him out of his leisurely mood. He straightened, pocketing his tobacco and pulling his hat down to shield his eyes.

"I should never have left," he said evenly. "Didn't settle anything. Just postponed it."

"Does it have to be settled?"

He shrugged. "I'll be able to answer that better after I talk to Dad."

"Jim." Impulsively she put a hand on his arm, eying him searchingly. "You'll be careful?"

Jim laughed, placing his hand over hers for a moment before drawing away. "Don't you worry, little one," he drawled. "I'll ride backward so nobody can get behind me."

He turned somewhat hurriedly and strode out, swinging onto his horse and reining toward the notch in the mountain without looking back. He had covered half a mile before he overcame his unreasonable feeling of being pursued.

"Hell's fire!" he breathed then. "I savvy now why that little rascal used to get so all fired on the prod. She's in love with me, just as shore as hell, and four years didn't change *her!*"

CHAPTER THREE

SHADOWS were lengthening by the time Jim rimmed out of the brushy, cottonwood-lined creek bed and came in sight of Five Drag headquarters. It was a beautiful spot, wild and lonely but infinitely satisfying. Jim, gazing at it now after four homesick years, understood perfectly why his dad had settled here. To a cowman drifting out of a war-ravaged Texas with a meager herd of cattle, a wife, and a baby son, this must have looked like heaven itself.

The squat adobe house and sprawling corrals were situated on a wide, oak-dotted bench at the mouth of the canyon, where the jagged mountain terrain gradually smoothed out to slope down to the flat expanse of the valley a thousand feet below. Involuntarily Jim turned for a look down the mesquite ridges, far across the shimmering country to the Caballo del Muerto range in the blue distance. Far out on the flat he could see the thick clump of cottonwoods that shielded the Ladder outfit, and his lips tightened grimly.

He had ridden slowly the five miles up from Pinal, often going out of his way to read brands and check on the condition of stock. The knowledge he had gained had added fuel to his smoldering anger.

He rode on to the corrals, noting with quick admiration the lean-limbed, prick-eared horses. He had begun to doubt that the men were at home, but the three saddles draped over the fence reassured him and he dismounted before the shed that served as a saddle room in stormy weather. He was automatically loosening his cinch when the clump of boots pulled him around.

A cowboy, as bowlegged as sixty years of riding could make him, had just come around the corner of the bunkhouse. Evidently he had not seen Jim ride in, as he was ambling forward with his eyes on the ground, his hat pulled low on his gray head.

Sight of the familiar figure brought a grin of pure joy to Jim's dark face. "Travelin' or goin' somewhere?" he drawled.

Dave's head jerked up as he stopped, his gray-green eyes squinted uncertainly. Then he threw up his hands with a wild shout. "Well, God!"

He rushed forward, grabbing Jim's hand with both of his and wringing it until it was numb. Dave Hurley and Long John Dixon had been pards long before the latter was married, and Dave had been like a second dad to Jim. Sight of the old man now, laughing and blinking rapidly against embarrassing tears, filled Jim with a wonderful glow.

"Dave, you old *bandalero*, it's shore good to see you. What do you know?"

"Nothin' worth tellin'." Dave stepped back, wiping the back of a gnarled hand over his face as he looked Jim up and down. "Doggone, cowboy," he said quizzically, "ain't you ever goin' to quit growin'?"

Jim laughed. "Shore, I've quit. Where's Dad?"

"In the house and shore achin' to see you. We didn't think you could make it so soon."

"I rustled," Jim admitted, sobering. "Couldn't be sure why Dad sent for me."

Dave's eyes narrowed with a reluctant, hard light. "Talked to anybody?"

"Several folks." Jim's grin was a little tight. "Donna Miller was the only one who was really glad to see me, and she was scared."

"Uh-huh," Dave said. "Reckon you didn't meet anybody from Ladder?"

"Rennick, anyhow."

Jim pulled off his hat and showed Dave the holes in the crown. The old man's eyes snapped with eagerness.

"Did you kill him?"

"Nope. He decided he didn't want to play."

"Not when you were watchin' for him, the damn snake! I figured Grant had boys watchin' the trails, Jim. He knew you were comin'."

"Yeah." Jim replaced his hat, avoiding Dave's penetrating gaze, but to no avail.

The old cowboy said shrewdly, "You saw Marilyn too, huh?"

"Yeah."

"And she took the hide off you."

Jim swung abruptly toward his horses, but Dave's hand on his arm stopped him.

"Now, don't stampede, young feller," he admonished. "You made that mistake once."

"It wouldn't have made any difference,' Jim said harshly.

"Well, you don't know much about women, but it's never too late to learn. You're still in love with her, ain't you?"

Jim cut him off with a furious gesture, glaring at the old cowboy but meeting nothing but a kindly interest in return. Suddenly he grinned.

"Damn you, Dave," he said mildly. "You talk too much."

"I'll do a lot of talkin' one of these days," Dave drawled imperturbably, "and you'll listen if I have to tie you down. Now you lope on over to the house and see the old man. I'll take care of these horses."

Jim went gladly enough, aware of a tingle in his veins that was not all eagerness to see his dad. Dave's keen words had hurt, but they had also aroused a burning curiosity. Jim recalled, with an unreasoning glow of pride, that Dave had always loved Marilyn and treated her as if she were his daughter. It was unlikely that the feeling between them had changed.

"Damn him!" he said again, with more fervency.

He quickened his stride, rounding the bunkhouse and bearing down on the back door of the old ranch house as if he were heading for a fight. He could hear the rasp of a meat saw as he let himself into the screened back porch, and the odor of frying potatoes and onions reminded him sharply that it had been some time since he'd eaten.

He didn't slacken his pace as he crossed the porch and entered the kitchen, but there he stopped, momentarily checked by the sight of his dad. Long John was bent over a quarter of beef, in the act of trading his saw for a wicked-looking butcher knife. His thinning hair, Jim noted, had turned white, and his gaunt frame was rounded at the shoulders. In years he was no older than Dave, but Jim realized poignantly that the years had hit him harder.

"Hey, you," he called gruffly. "Need a cook?"

Long John recognized the voice. The knife flew out of his hand as he spun around, stumbling against the table in his haste. For a moment he stared, as if to confirm his doubting senses. Then a spark flew into his tired gray eyes, and a broad smile wreathed his lined face.

"Jim, you son-of-a-gun! Sneakin' up behind the old man!"

He stepped forward with both hands extended and Jim met him halfway, shaking hands and embracing him at the same time.

"Dad, how are you?"

"Fine—now. Golly, boy, I'm glad to see you!"

"Well, that shore goes double." Jim stepped back, his hands still on his dad's shoulders, grinning like a schoolboy under the old man's shining eyes. "Been a hell of a long time, hasn't it?"

"A *long* time. What all you been doin,' son?"

A little bit of everything. Mining, punchin' cows, runnin' horses. I had a fair-to-middlin' horse ranch when I got your message."

He unbuttoned his shirt and removed a heavy money belt from around his waist, weighed it in his hand for a moment, then handed it to his dad, laughing at the old man's bulging stare.

"My gosh, Jim, where'd you get all this?"

"Worked for it," Jim said with pardonable pride. "There's around five thousand there."

"Jim—" Long John hesitated. "I've heard stories—about gun-play. You've been goin' straight, haven't you, son?"

"Dad, I've shore been goin' straight," Jim said forcefully. "I took a deputy marshal's badge for a while up in Montana and again over in Idaho. I had to use a gun more than once on those jobs, but it wasn't because I wanted to. As soon as I got a stake, I started buildin' up a horse herd. I brought one of the wild bunch home with me, a sorrel named El Capitán; and if you don't try to steal him from me, then you're losin' your eyesight."

John's grin came back as he hefted the belt and said, "Those horses up there must be worth money."

"Between a hundred and two hundred dollars apiece, broke. I could have got more for Cappy than any of the rest, but I couldn't sell him. Wait'll you see him, Dad. Best horse I ever forked."

"Uh-huh. Jim, you're not—sorry I sent for you?"

"Hell, no! I been wantin' to come home, but—you know—"

"Yeah." John looked down at the belt in his hands and rubbed a big thumb over it absently. "Things have grown kinda bad around here."

"Since Old Man Talbot died?"

"Yeah."

Jim studied his dad's face, reluctant to put his question into words. No cowman liked to call a neighbor a thief, no matter how hard his personal feelings might be. "I saw an awful lot of cattle comin' up through the brush," he said finally, "but darn few Five Drags."

"Darn few," John agreed grimly, "and even fewer Bells and Lazy L. You remember the Lathrops down on the flat and the Bells on the creek?"

"Shore. I saw two little kids at Bells' as I came by. They looked kinda ragged."

"Did you notice anything else?"

"Yes, I did," Jim said slowly. "What stock we've got down there is dry cows or cows with baby calves. I never saw one damn yearling or two-year-old that wasn't branded Ladder!"

Long John punctuated that remark by slamming the heavy belt onto the table. "You won't see one, either."

"How come?"

Long John pulled in a deep breath and then held it, staring hard at the floor. Jim, waiting, rolled a cigarette, wondering bleakly if it was his fault the Bell children were ragged. Marilyn had said "that kind of trouble" was never forgotten, and Grant hadn't been able to get his hands on the man he wanted.

"Jim—" Long John's gaze was deeply thoughtful. "You left here a wild-eyed kid and you've come back a hardeyed man. I hope to God I didn't do wrong in sending for you."

"It's that bad, huh?" Jim said evenly.

John nodded heavily. "I wanted you here, Jim, but if anything happens to you—"

"Hell!" Jim tossed his hat onto a chair and turned to the washbasin. "We'll worry about something happenin' to me when it happens. Let's eat and then we'll talk. I shore got a lot of questions."

For several moments after Dave and Ramón had left the house, Jim and his dad sat smoking in silence, facing each other across the narrow table. The meal had been a merry one, with no mention of the current trouble; and Jim, with his long legs stretched under the table and a kerosene lamp burning cheer-fully at his elbow, realized the full comfort of being home even if times were hard.

And he had no doubt of his welcome, here at Five Drag. Ramón, a leathery-faced, black-eyed Yaqui, had been as pitifully glad to see him as his dad and Dave had been. The old *vaquero* had ridden for Five Drag for over fifteen years and could be counted on to stick, regardless.

"What happened to the other boys?" Jim asked suddenly.

"Billy and Hank are buried up here on the bench where Mother is."

"Who did it?"

It was significant that Jim did not ask what had happened to them.

Long John shook his head. "Those thirty-thirty slugs didn't have return addresses on 'em, Jim. And Pecos just disappeared. We never did find him. The others quit, and I reckon you can't blame 'em. Thirty bucks a month ain't much to go to hell for."

"Dave and Ramón didn't quit," Jim said pointedly.

"Oh, no, and they haven't been getting anything but grub this last year, either."

"Had anybody threatened the boys, warned 'em to get out?"

"Not that I know of. Not in so many words, anyhow."

"That's answer enough," Jim said grimly. "How long you three old badgers been runnin' this place by yourselves?"

"Two years, and they've shore been rough ones. The water holes all went dry and even Talbot's *ciénaga* down on the flat got so low at times that it wouldn't water their stock. They've been drivin' up through here to get at our spring."

"And I reckon the boys objected to that?"

"Some."

Jim really had his answer now. In good years Deep Creek, heading at the spring up the canyon, ran far down into the flat; but in bad years the runoff wouldn't carry much below the ranch headquarters. Five Drag couldn't afford either the water or the grass necessary to support all the cattle Ladder could shove onto it.

"How many hands has Grant got?"

"Hard to tell," Long John replied with a dubious shake of his head. "He's got men comin' and goin' all the time, but I reckon he's got at least twelve or fifteen steady. That's an awful big outfit now, Jim."

"Ought to be," Jim said bluntly, "if they've been helpin' themselves to every calf that dropped!"

"Well, we can't prove they have," John said cautiously. "Grant claims to have bought a lot of young stuff, and he claims the rustlers have been gettin' ours. You know, we've always had a little trouble with rustlers, and these last few years, there's been an awful lot of riffraff driftin' into the country. Outlaws of all kinds—stage robbers, gunmen, rustlers."

"But they're not bothering Ladder!"

"No-o-o. Ladder's too strong, for one thing, and they're gettin' stronger every day. They've bought up all the little outfits on the other side of the valley, and they're after us over here awful heavy. I'd see Grant in hell before I'd sell to him, but these other fellas—Holmes and Smith and Bell and Lathrop—they're busted, Jim. And they've all got families. I talked 'em into holdin' off till you got here. Thought maybe if we ganged up we could hold out till better times."

"What you mean," Jim said deliberately, "is that maybe we can hold our own against Grant Talbot."

"Now, Jim, don't look like that, damnit! We've got to play it careful. Someday the law will be strong enough out here to—"

Jim cut him off with a sharp gesture. "Just how come we haven't got any young stuff?"

"Two years ago Grant claimed that all us fellers on this side of the valley were stealin' from *him*, and he barred us from roundup."

"Barred you?" Jim straightened, eying his dad incredulously. "You mean you haven't cut a herd down there on the flat for two years?"

"That's right."

"Why, the dirty—" Jim broke off, again stung by the feeling that this was all his fault. "It's me Grant's hittin' at. I should never have left."

"Well, son, you couldn't tell. You were tryin' to avoid trouble, and I always admired you for it. Then there was Marilyn."

Again Jim cut him off. "How many cattle have we got now?"

John threw up his hands. "God knows. I don't. Three of us couldn't do the ridin'."

"Why in hell didn't you send for me sooner?" Jim demanded.

Long John made a helpless little gesture, then said simply, "I was afraid to, son. I knew Grant would be after you for what happened to Dick, and he's got too many men. But now—He's gettin' stronger all the time, and if you want the old home ranch, I reckon now's the time to fight for it."

"You know damn well I want it!" Jim said hotly. "And even if I didn't, do you think I'd let Grant Talbot take it way from you?"

"Well, son, it's sure good to hear you." John's smile was wistful. "Your mother and I worked awful hard, buildin' up this spread, and we had our dreams. You know, someday Arizona will be a heaven on earth for decent folks. It's big and it's beautiful and it's got everything a man could want. Right now it's a dump ground for the whole damn country, but times like these can't last. When the country does grow up, I'd shore like to think there'd be a Five Drag cow in it."

"There will be," Jim said grimly, "or else there'll be a lot more graves up there on the bench!"

Abruptly he stood up and stepped away from his chair, thinking to walk outside and try to smooth his tangled emotions. His feeling for the old home ranch, his hatred of Grant Talbot, his love for Marilyn, which was a steady, nagging ache somewhere inside him....

He heard the bullet strike, a terrible sodden sound, even before the glass shattered out of the window behind him. Then came the heavy report of a rifle from out in the dark. For a second Jim stood frozen, staring at the widening bloodstain on the front of his dad's shirt. Then, with one sweep of his hand, he knocked the lamp from the table and plunged the room into darkness.

CHAPTER FOUR

I N THE sudden blackness Jim sprang around the table, feeling for his dad and catching him as the old man slumped out of his chair. Jim eased him to the floor, hearing the harsh rasp of his breathing, feeling the weakness in the fingers that groped at him.

A brief riot of sound filled the night outside. Several shrill yells mingled with the pound of hoofs and the crash of guns. Then silence, broken only by the uneven thump of running feet. The back door screeched as it was flung open, and Dave's urgent voice shot through the darkness.

"John! Jim! What happened?"

"Fetch a lamp," Jim snapped. "Ramón, ride for the doctor. Dad's hit."

"They steal the horses," Ramón said in his soft voice that nothing could ruffle. "Ever' damn one. But I run to Bells' and get one."

He said the last of it as he was hurrying out the door. Dave was already stumbling around the kitchen, trying to find a lamp, swearing in a steady, vicious monotone. Jim tore at his dad's shirt, getting it open, feeling with trembling hand for the wound. When he found it, low in the chest, an icy fear clamped down on him; but he kept it out of his voice.

"Take it easy, Dad. We'll have this fixed in no time."

When Dave came with the lamp, however, Jim's fear turned into an agony of helplessness. All the patching in the world couldn't keep John Dixon's life from seeping out through the hole under his heart. The old man's eyes were open, and his lips twitched into a weary smile.

"I was afraid the old bench was due for some new customers," he said huskily. "I was—afraid it'd be you."

"That slug was meant for me!" Jim burst out. "If I hadn't moved—"

"My life wouldn't have been worth living, anyhow. It's all right, son."

"I'll kill him!" Jim gritted with icy passion. "Ill shoot his goddamned heart out!"

"Listen, Jim." Anxiety flitted across John's face and then smoothed out into a quiet resignation. "You were right a while ago. I did call you home to help us fight Grant Talbot. Someone's got to stop him for the good of the whole country, and none of us could do it. I hope to God you can, but take it slow."

He had to pause, closing his eyes against the pain. When he looked up again, he pulled his breath in slowly and parceled his words out with infinite care.

"Get the proof against him before you do anything, Jim. Stay inside the law. Remember, you're building a country for decent folks, and you can't do it by running wild with a gun. Promise me you won't go after him—"

"Dad—" Jim protested desperately.

"Wait, son." John's voice was growing weaker, but he kept on doggedly. "It's your Five Drag now. It's been a good old ranch, clean and square, and I'd like to think you'll keep it that way. Give me your promise that you'll get the deadwood on Grant before you go after him. Then—get him."

"You've got it!"

"That makes it easier."

Long John seemed to relax, letting go of himself with a tired sigh. Dave grabbed his hand.

"John, don't quit," he said tersely. "You can make it, pard, if you try."

"Not this time, Dave. You—take care of this—kid of mine."
The old rancher shifted his dimming glance back to Jim, taking a long, searching look that would have to last him. Then he
smiled, fumbling for Jim's hand and gripping it with the last of
his failing strength. "I'm—shore glad—you got here. God, I hate
to leave now."

Jim never knew how long he knelt there, gripping his father's
hand. He was aware that Dave shoved to his feet and stumbled
out of the room, but it was some time afterward that Jim lifted
his dad and carried him into the front bedroom. He covered
him gently, as he would have a sleeping child, then turned back
through the house and stalked outside.

He paused in the dark to roll and smoke a cigarette, gazing
long at the remotely twinkling stars and gradually finding ease
for his aching throat. The war was on, and first blood went to
Ladder. But it would not be the last.

With his thoughts hardening into a relentless purpose, Jim
walked to the bunkhouse. A lamp burned fitfully on the cluttered table and beside it sat Dave, his head bent low over the gun
he was cleaning.

Jim glanced somberly around the long, low building. He
remembered it as being filled with bedrolls, riding gear, banter-
ing cowboys. Now it was like an empty barn, hauntingly silent,
with only two of the bunks ranging around the walls showing
occupancy.

Jim dropped onto an empty bunk near Dave and rolled
another cigarette. The old cowboy did not look up from his task,
nor did Jim want him to. He had seen Dave's eyes in the kitchen,
seen them go flat and grow old in the space of a second.

"Shore." Dave's voice was rough, almost curt. "There was
at least two fellers by the corral, maybe three. They headed the
horses for Devil's Pass."

"Did you find anything at all that would pin them down?"
"No."

"So they got away clean." Jim's voice grew edged in spite of the iron grip he had on himself. "They shore had it timed. They must have had the gate open before that other man fired."

"Yeah. Left us afoot!" Dave's hands trembled as he rammed the cloth through the barrel of his .45. "I couldn't hit a damn thing tonight, but by God, I won't be shootin' in the dark next time."

His actions said more plainly than words that he was primed to shoot on sight, and Jim said in an even tone, "We've got to make shore."

"I am shore!" Dave said hotly, jerking his head up and slamming his glittering eyes at Jim. "There's only one man I'm gunnin' for. Grant Talbot!"

"We've got to get the proof, Dave. I promised Dad."

"I didn't make no promises, and I shore as hell don't have to prove what I already know."

"It might have been Rennick," Jim said evenly. "He tried to kill me once before."

"That don't change anything! Rennick's not doin' anything Grant doesn't tell him to do." Dave wiped the gun carefully before starting to shove fresh loads into it. His voice shook. "They were tryin' to break John quick, before he could get these other fellers organized. I reckon they were afraid now you're here that you'd get the job done."

"They had a right to be scared," Jim said grimly. "I'll see Bell and the others in the morning. Then we'll all look for proof."

"Well, while you're lookin', I'm gonna be shootin'. It's Ladder we're fightin', cowboy, and don't you forget it!"

"I'm not going to forget it,' Jim said, his voice suddenly hard, "but we're going to get the goods on 'em before we do anything. Then *I'm* going to do it."

"You're gonna have help," Dave said stubbornly.

"You heard me, Dave." Jim came off the bunk and stepped forward, his fist unconsciously doubled. "You heard the promise

I made Dad—to take it slow and get the proof. Until I do get it, Grant Talbot's my meat, and you lay off him!"

Slowly Dave came to his feet and slipped the gun into his holster. Just as slowly the defiant glare in his eyes melted before a grim smile. "Jim, I've seen your dad look like that, many's the time, and it was too late to duck. All right, son. You're the boss, but I'll be right behind you."

"Thanks, Dave."

Jim hesitated, wanting to soften the harshness of his ultimatum, but words wouldn't come. He finally gave up, dropping his hand on the old cowboy's shoulder for a brief moment before turning back out into the night.

They buried Long John Dixon the next morning, on the grassy bench across the creek. Jim, his spurs on his boots and his gun belt sagging around his waist, turned away in stony silence when the job was done, heading back for the house.

Donna Miller turned with him, keeping her thoughts to herself but telling him by her nearness that those thoughts were of him. Jim had been surprised and pleased when Donna and her father drove up, having been told of the tragedy by old Doc Adams. The four ranchers Jim wanted to talk to had come also, with their families.

Their presence was comforting, but Jim found himself wondering bleakly if Marilyn had heard of this murder, wondering what her reaction would be. He thought bitterly, I reckon we're even now.

To Donna, he said gruffly, "Does this answer your question?"

She lifted her head quickly, her dark eyes soft and luminous beneath her blue bonnet. "What question?"

"About whether or not this has got to be settled."

Judge Miller, beyond her, cleared his throat uncomfortably. He was a medium-sized man, heavy around the waist, with pale blue eyes squinted behind his spectacles and with a tight-lipped mouth above his jutting chin. Where he got his title no one remembered, but it was a cinch he had never presided over any court.

"You know who did it, Jim?" he asked uneasily.

"Don't you?" Jim shot back at him.

"No," the Judge said carefully, "I don't. There are a lot of people running loose in this country who'd kill a man for a corralful of good horses."

"Maybe," Jim retorted, "and maybe there are a few people running loose who'd steal a corralful of horses just to kill their tracks."

"Could be," the Judge admitted, then added without emphasis, "Skeet Dorman's a friend of yours, but he's an awful square lawman."

Jim glanced over at him sharply. The Judge met his eyes for only a brief moment, but his warning was clear enough.

"Thanks, Judge, but there's no call to worry," Jim drawled, warming a little to this evidence of friendship. "I may kill me a skunk or two, but I'll make darn shore I don't have to swing for it."

The ranch yard, crowded with wagons and buckboards, looked deceptively placid in the midmorning sunlight. As the group approached, the four ranch women moved in stolid silence to their respective vehicles, pulling their solemn-eyed, shiny-faced children with them. Jim helped Donna into her buckboard, secretly glad that the Judge had refused his invitation to stay a while. The other men, he noticed, were gravitating toward the corrals, and he was impatient to join them.

"Thanks for coming," he said simply.

Donna smiled as she held out her hand. "We wanted to, Jim. Come in for dinner sometime."

"Thanks, but I reckon I may be pretty busy."

"If there's anything I can do to help you—'

Jim, aware of the Judge's narrow scrutiny, squeezed her hand and stepped back. "You better stick to tendin' store, young lady," he said evenly, "but I'll remember your offer."

He touched his hat brim and nodded politely before turning away, hearing the abrupt snap of the Judge's whip. Judge Miller might be willing to offer a reserved friendship, but he was not willing to offer his daughter, and Jim couldn't blame him. The odds were too great that she would, one way or another, get hurt.

Jim had to pass the Bell wagon on his way around the house. He looked up, intending to speak, but Mrs. Bell had her head lowered, brushing at lint on the front of her gray cotton dress. Deliberately, it seemed to Jim, she avoided his glance; and he headed for the corrals with a mounting drive inside him.

Ramón and Dave sat side by side with their backs against the pole fence, several feet away from the spreading oak where the other four men hunkered in the shade. All of the men had their heads lowered, smoking in thoughtful silence.

Jim came to a slow halt near them, sensing a strain that could not all have been caused by the recent funeral. He rolled a cigarette, studying them for several moments before asking quietly, "When's Ladder planning to round up?"

There was a marked pause in which Holmes, Smith, and Lathrop all looked at Bell. He was a rawboned man with a long, homely face and a sandy-colored beard.

"They started three days ago," he said slowly. "Got a big herd bunched down on the flat now."

"Yeah?" Jim's grim satisfaction didn't show in his voice. He was uncertain o<a> his status with these men, feeling his way through their obvious reluctance to talk. "Dad told me what kind of time you fellas been havin' around here. I reckon maybe that's my fault."

"Naw, hell!" The rancher's negative gesture held supreme disgust. "Grant's a hog, that's all, and poison mean on top of it."

Thus reassured, Jim hunkered down on his spurs and shoved his hat to the back of his head. "How many cattle you men runnin' now?"

Holmes laughed bitterly. "Plenty, if we could collect the yearlings and weaners wearing a Ladder brand. Damn few, if you don't count them."

"None of us know for sure, Jim," Bell added. "We haven't been doin' much ridin' lately. Just waitin'."

"Dad talked to you, didn't he, about gangin' together to see what we could do?"

"Yeah, that's all he has talked about lately. Wait for Jim to come."

Jim hesitated, wondering at the queer inflection in Bell's voice. Smith and Lathrop still hadn't looked up, their faces hidden behind their lowered hat brims, and Jim again directed his question to Bell.

"Where does Brady fit into this?"

"He doesn't fit. His Bar X is away down in the canyon and nobody's bothered him—yet, anyway."

"Yeah, he's gettin' his own cattle out of it, but he's tendin' to his own business awful close."

"He might come in with us," Jim said thoughtfully. "He ought to be able to see that if we go under he'll be next."

"That's poor figurin'," Holmes said bluntly. "He's got half a dozen men workin' for him, and he don't want any part of Grant Talbot."

"Well, hell," Jim said, getting edgy, "there's seven of us, too. How many men is it going to take to lick Ladder?"

"More than we've got," Bell said flatly, "and more than we can get. We're scattered, Jim. We haven't got the chance of a rabbit in the middle of a wolf pack, and I've had enough."

"Enough?" Jim echoed incredulously. "You mean you're quittin'?"

"Quittin' cold. We talked it over last night and decided to pull out."

Slowly Jim got to his feet, dropping his cigarette and fanning the smoke away from his face. Now that it was out, the ranchers were all looking at him, but their eyes wouldn't hold before his piercing glare.

"Long John said to wait for you," Bell pointed out defensively, "and all it got him was a slug. This thing's changin' now, Jim. I had a hunch but I was willing to wait, to see. Grant has been just crowdin', quiet like, but from here on he's going to be shootin'. Last night proves that. He hates your guts, and he'll be gunnin' for anybody that sides you. No, sir." He shook his head emphatically. "Count me out."

"Both of us," Holmes grunted, and the other two ranchers muttered their agreement.

"So you're pullin' out, are you?" Jim said acidly. "Runnin' before the fight even starts!"

"The fight's been going on for three years," Holmes retorted with heat. "We were licked before you ever came and now it'll get worse. I'll be damned if I want to wake up some mornin' with a slug in *my* back!"

"You'd better come with us, Jim," Bell said earnestly. "All you'll ever get around here is the same thing your father got."

"Might be," Jim said, spacing his words deliberately, "but by God, I'd rather get it than to tuck my tail!"

Holmes lunged to his feet, his face flushing with anger. "You can drop that yellow chatter, Dixon. You haven't got anybody to think about but your own damn self. I've got a wife and kids, and I'll be damned if I'm interested in having a widow and a bunch of orphans. You can stay here and go to hell if you want to. I'm goin' over on the Gila, and I'm startin' right now!"

He swung toward his companions, challenging them with a blazing stare. Smith and Lathrop lost no time in getting to their feet, but Bell came up slowly, his face showing red above his beard. Evidently he had been chosen as spokesman, and he obviously regretted the fact that the conference had got out of hand.

As Holmes started past him, Jim threw out an arm to stop him. "Wait," he said shortly. Then he waited himself, calling to mind the four ranches these men were abandoning.

Holmes had settled at the far north end of the valley, near the end of the Pinal range, in a rugged canyon that controlled the only water in the area. Smith's place was closer, over a ridge to the north and west of Five Drag. Lathrop's Lazy L was down on the flat, almost due west of Five Drag, while Bell was on the creek to the south and west. The four places formed a semicircle that hemmed Five Drag in, its back to the mountain.

The strips of land they had title to were but specks in the vast sweep of the range, but they commanded the use of that range. Or would command it in the days ahead when disputes could be settled by courts instead of six-guns.

"I reckon I owe you fellas an apology," Jim said slowly. "I don't blame you for gettin' out while you can. This is no country for women and kids—yet."

"Jim, I hate like the devil to go," Bell replied, and Jim couldn't doubt his sincerity. "Not leavin' the ranch so much. There's nothin' much in that but <a> few years' work, and I got more; but I hate the idea of leavin' you here to fight that outfit alone."

"Who in hell said he was alone?"

Jim swung toward the sound of the gruff voice to find Dave and Ramón, still side by side but now on their feet, leaning back against the corral with their thumbs hooked in their cartridge belts, their hats pulled down hard over their narrowed eyes.

"Me," Dave said evenly, "I ain't goin' nowhere."

"Me, too," the Yaqui echoed in his soft voice. "I stay here. Aboveground or underneath."

He shrugged, an expressive gesture that thrilled Jim as much as their words.

"Three of you," Holmes mused, "against the whole damn valley. Hell! It'll be underneath, cowboy, and don't you ever doubt it."

"Could be," Jim said, his confidence rising, "but we're not planted yet. What you men going to do with your places?"

"That's what hurts the worst," Bell mumbled apologetically. "We've got to have a little money to get out of the country on, Jim. That means we'll have to sell—to Ladder."

"How much is Grant offerin'?"

"Five hundred."

"Five hundred!" The paltry offer astounded Jim and confirmed beyond a doubt the ranchers' statements that they were broke, licked. "Well," he said dryly, "I reckon you couldn't expect Grant to offer to pay for the cattle when he can get 'em for nothin' with a runnin' iron. I'll give you a thousand, cash on the barrelhead."

For a moment no one spoke. Then Bell said constrainedly, "Jim, you feelin' all right?"

Jim couldn't help grinning at their awed expressions. "Come on in the house," he said, speaking naturally for the first time that day. "We'll draw up the bills of sale before I lose my nerve. With five ranches on my string, I'm apt to die an important man, don't you know it?"

When the bills of sale were completed, Jim had only one request to make of the departing ranchers. "Keep this deal under your hats, will you? I might live longer if Grant doesn't know I beat him to those places. Besides, I'd kinda like the pleasure of tellin' him myself."

"We won't say a doggone word to anybody," Bell assured him gratefully.

Holmes added, "I'm not even going to stop to say good-by. Old Man Gila, here I come!"

Long after they had gone, Jim stood idly staring out the window, their wishes for good luck still ringing in his ears. He would need all the good luck he could round up, but he had committed himself and did not regret it. His dad, he thought somberly, would have been pleased at this.

Remembering that his dad had said Ramón and Dave had not been paid for a year, he picked up his lightened money belt and strode back out through the kitchen. He noted that some of the womenfolk had straightened the room, washing the dishes and removing the glass and stains from the broken lamp. Then he saw the cluster of strange, cloth-covered dishes on the table and found that they contained enough cooked food to last for several days. Bread, a pot of beans, a pan of roast meat. Even a chocolate cake.

Trust a woman, he thought with a queer tingle of pleasure, to look after a man's stomach when he's forgotten it himself.

And he wondered if any of those various dishes had been prepared by Donna Miller. He looked again at the chocolate cake, the icing spread to a satiny smoothness, and nodded, smiling to himself.

"Sure as you're born," he murmured. "The little devil."

Thought of Donna inevitably brought its comparison with Marilyn, and he stalked on out the back door with stiffening lips. Dave and Ramón were in the near corral, peering off over the rough mesquite ridges toward Devil's Pass. Jim, following their gaze, tried to see what they were looking at so intently; but before he could locate it, a rider came around the corner of the saddle shed and pulled to a halt. Jim whirled at the sound of the horse, but he stopped short as he saw that the rider was Marilyn Talbot.

Her glance touched him hurriedly before going on to Dave, who had swung around and was approaching somewhat uncertainly. Ramón, without a word, lifted his hat to her, set it back on his head at precisely the same angle, and strolled away toward the bunkhouse.

Jim leaned back against the snubbing post and rolled a cigarette, watching a dull red flush creep up Marilyn's neck to flood her face.

"Howdy, Marilyn," Dave said with constraint. "You lost?"

"No, I—" Her eyes flicked to Jim, flicked back to Dave as she shifted uncomfortably in the saddle. 'Uncle Dave, I just wanted to tell you how sorry I am about all this. I know how it feels to—lose someone you love very much."

"Why, honey, it was sweet of you to ride over," Dave returned, surprised and pleased. "It has been kind of rough."

He rested his hand on the fork of her saddle and she quickly covered it. Or tried to. Her little hand, Jim saw, was sadly inadequate.

"Uncle Dave, is there anything at all I can do to help you?"

"Reckon not. Things like this, a feller kinda has to do for himself."

"Of course."

Jim wanted to leave. The fact that she was absolutely ignoring him while voicing a heartfelt sympathy for Dave was eating into him like a bad case of screw worms, but a stubborn defiance held him against the post. He had wondered what her reaction would be. He was finding out, but he could not have prepared himself for her next question.

"Do you have any idea who did it?"

Dave ducked his head, rubbing the back of his neck as if he had just been stung by a bee. "They—got clean away," he said haltingly. "Never left no sign, that we've found so far, anyhow."

Jim shoved abruptly away from the post and lounged forward, cuffing his hat impudently far over his right eye. He saw the guard fly up in her eyes but he tilted his head back, hands on hips, and regarded her steadily for several moments before asking in a cool drawl, "Where was Grant last night?"

CHAPTER FIVE

MARILYN made no immediate move to answer. She glanced at Dave, then turned back to Jim with such a carefully impersonal stare that a cold, tight fury closed in on him.

"Embarrassing question, huh?" he said, with a challenging lift to his voice. "Shore a man isn't supposed to embarrass a beautiful woman, but I'll risk it again. Was Grant home last night?"

"Certainly he was home," she snapped.

"Did he get home ahead of you?"

"No, but—"

"Didn't go straight home from town, huh?"

"No, but that's not—"

"Just what time did he get home?"

Marilyn jerked erect in her saddle. "I don't know exactly," she said hotly, "but that's got nothing to do with you."

"Oh, shore not," Jim drawled with a sarcastic ring. "I'm just curious, that's all. You say he was home, but you don't know what time he got there. Where *was* your darlin' brother last night, honey?"

"Jim—" Dave cut in, lifting an anxious hand.

"Back up, Dave." Jim was still drawling, although his voice had taken on the sharp edge of a skinning knife. Not for anything in the world would he let her know she had hurt him, but he couldn't help his savage desire to hurt her in turn. "I'm askin' the questions this trip, and kinda looks like the little lady is havin' trouble answerin' 'em."

"I've answered them," Marilyn said flatly. "Even if I can't tell you the exact minute Grant walked into the house, I can tell you that he wasn't over here. He's no murderer!"

"He isn't, huh? Well, I'm glad to hear it."

Jim's tone gave the lie to his words; and Marilyn's breast heaved as she pulled in a deep breath, her red lips making a straight line across her face. Jim thought remotely that she was never more beautiful than when she was mad.

"I figured you'd come up with an idea like this," she said. "That's why I hesitated about coming over here, but I couldn't let Uncle Dave think I'd forgotten him."

"I know, Marilyn," Dave said hastily. "I'm—"

"It's all right, Uncle Dave. You can't help this." She looked again at Jim, her eyes flashing like blue lightning as they swept over him. "I'm sorry about your dad," she said then, deliberately. "He was a good man, and it's too bad you can't be more like him."

Jim felt his face tighten, but he retorted coolly, "Reckon I'm not so different. Dad wouldn't have let Grant run over him, either, if he'd been younger."

"Grant's not running over anybody!" she burst out, her anger flaring beyond bounds. "If he gets hard once in a while, it's because he has to. You can't run a ranch in this country by being soft-handed. Grant's good and clean and decent!"

Her eyes said plainly enough that she didn't expect him to understand the meaning of the word decent; and Jim spat suddenly, as if he'd just bitten into a piece of rancid bacon. Then he took a slow stride forward, his fists unconsciously knotted. "Maybe he's nice and clean and decent," he said, biting the words out, "but from here on he'll have to confine his brandin' to his own calves. We're cuttin' that roundup tomorrow!"

For a moment Marilyn sat rigid, her nostrils flaring with restrained fury at the accusation. Then she wheeled her horse and spurred him into a headlong run toward the trail to town.

Jim, watching her go, was aware that Dave was mopping his face with a sleeve, looking at him with undisguised consternation.

"For God's sake, Jim—"

Jim said tightly, "Look out, Dave."

Dave held his breath for a second, then let it out carefully. "Yeah," he murmured. He wiped his face again, pulled his hat down hard over his eyes, and squinted off down the country at the spot where Marilyn had disappeared.

Jim looked beyond that spot, far out on the flats where the giant cottonwoods guarded the Ladder headquarters, aware of a tightness in his chest that made breathing difficult. His desire to hurt Marilyn had backfired.

He started to lift his hands automatically for tobacco, and only then did he realize he still held the money belt. He glanced sidelong at Dave. The old cowboy was still avoiding his gaze, and Jim slapped the belt around his waist and jerked it tight. That settlement would have to wait.

Presently Dave sighed and said, with an attempt at being matter-of-fact, "Wonder if Ramón's got those horses yet."

"Horses?" Jim echoed, jarred out of his thoughts.

"Yeah. We thought we saw old Pete and Rusty comin' back. We've been grainin' those two old fellers pretty regular, and it'd shore take a good pair of hobbles to keep 'em away from here."

Without a word Jim whirled and strode rapidly to the saddle shed, grabbing the rope off his saddle. He hadn't, until now, had either the time or the inclination to worry about being afoot; but the prospect of getting a horse under him and taking the trail of his remuda fitted perfectly with his violent mood.

He still had a hunch that the horses had been taken merely to cover the tracks of the bushwhackers and prevent pursuit. This seemed proved when he and Dave found the rest of the animals scattered and grazing in a sheltered, oak-studded bowl next to the mountain. Jim was relieved to find Cappy and the dun with them. The two horses had evidently been too hungry and weary to drift, even though the range was new to them.

"Coyote trick," Dave grunted. "Run 'em off just to set us afoot and then turn 'em loose."

"Shore," Jim said shortly. "You didn't think he could afford to get caught with 'em, did you?"

By the time they got back to the corral, he had worked off most of the black, savage mood that was riding him. He and Dave unsaddled Pete and Rusty and turned them into the bunch, then strode slowly back to the saddle shed, where Ramón hunkered in the shade mending a stirrup strap.

Jim pulled the money belt from around his waist. "Dad said you fellas hadn't been paid for a long time. How much you got comin'?"

"Nothin'," Dave said flatly.

"Nothin'?" Jim echoed. "Dad said it'd been a year."

"You don't owe me one damn cent," Dave said emphatically. "I'll take my pay in Ladder hides."

Jim glanced down at Ramón, hesitating. The old Yaqui didn't look up. He merely flipped the stirrup leather he was mending so that Jim could see the Five Drag brand that had been burned into the leather. At the same time Dave pulled a brown leather wallet out of his pocket and extended it so that Jim could see the Five Drag that had been burned into that, too.

"Marilyn made that for me," he said with pride, "last Christmas."

Jim looked quickly down at the belt in his hands. Their answers had been plain enough. This was their outfit, and all they wanted was a chance to fight for it. Abruptly he tossed the belt onto the fence, feeling a tight gratitude that he couldn't express.

"Well," he said gruffly, "we may get licked, but by God, we'll leave some marks to show for it!"

Shadows were growing long in the corral by the time the men finished their preparations for the roundup. Dave and Ramón had all the gear mended and ready and were now cleaning their rifles with reverent care. Jim had just finished shoeing the third horse, straightening gratefully and reaching for a long delayed cigarette, when Eddie Worthington and Skeet Dorman rode up. They were dusty, sober-faced, with a suggestion of fatigue in the way they sat their saddles.

"Howdy," Jim said, laying his left arm over the neck of the horse he had just shod. "Pile off and rest your saddles."

Eddie wrapped the reins around his saddle horn and reached for tobacco; but Dorman dismounted stiffly, coming straight to Jim and extending his hand.

"Jim, I'm shore sorry."

"Thanks, Skeet," Jim replied with constraint. "I expected you out before this."

"Hell! Last night's the first time in forty years that I went to bed early. Nobody thought to look for me there." He paused, nodding to Dave and Ramón before asking, "Did you find anything at all that would pin it on anybody?"

"Not a thing." Jim still wondered what had kept him from coming out earlier in the day, but he didn't ask, turning his attention instead to Eddie. "Shade don't cost any more than the sunshine does," he invited, gesturing toward the shadow in which Dave and Ramón were seated.

Eddie dismounted slowly and lounged forward, his eyes not on Jim but on Dave. Jim flashed a look at Dave, wondering, but the old cowboy was concentrating studiously on the carbine he was cleaning.

Dorman cuffed his hat over his left ear and scratched the back of his head. "You fellers aimin' to fight the Civil War over again?" he inquired, and the tone of his voice asked a good deal more than did his actual words.

"Might be more like a revolution," Jim replied. "There's gonna be some changes made." He paused, then added carelessly, "We're cuttin' Grant's herd tomorrow."

"Oh, yeah?" Dorman eyed Jim searchingly for a moment, then flicked another glance at the rifles, grinning faintly. "Time was," he murmured, "when it was the chuck wagon that got oiled before a roundup. Bell and those other three fellas ridin' with you?"

"Nope. They pulled out."

"Aw! Sold out to Grant?"

"Nope." Jim could not restrain a grin. "Sold out to me."

There was an instant of absolute silence, during which Dorman stared at him, wide-eyed. Then Eddie laughed suddenly.

"Mammal" he exclaimed, his brown eyes dancing with an unholy glee. "Old Grant's just plain goin' to bite himself!"

"Yeah," Dorman said slowly, "if he don't bite Jim first. Damn, Jim, I wish you'd bought those places yesterday."

"Why?"

Dorman shifted uncomfortably, once more scratching the back of his head. Jim, turning a questioning glance to Eddie, saw the cowboy's face go very still.

"What's up?" Jim demanded.

Dorman looked up reluctantly. "Don't reckon you fellas been off the place, have you?"

"Dave and I rode over here a ways to round up the horses. That's all."

"Then I reckon you ain't heard that the Fort Irby stage was held up last night."

"Where?"

"Out here beyond Smith's place. One of the Bar X boys comin' up from the canyon this mornin' found it. Driver and guard both dead. I was just gettin' ready to come out here when I heard about it, so Eddie and I rode out to take a look." Dorman turned partly away, spat into the corral dust, then added without inflection, "Three men did the job. We trailed 'em this far."

Jim stood rock still for a moment, stunned. He was aware that Dave and Ramón were shoving to their feet, but he kept his eyes glued to Dorman's lined face. Then his shock gave way to a blazing anger.

"So I robbed the stage, did I?" he burst out, slamming his cigarette to the ground. "Killed my own dad and ran off my own horses to cover my trail!"

"Now, don't go off half-cocked, young feller. I'm just tellin' you what folks might think"

"I don't give a damn what they think! I worked for that money; and if you don't believe it, you can damn well write and check up on it!"

"Listen, you hotheaded maverick," Dorman said forcefully. "I've knowed your dad too long to ever believe he sired a stage robber, and I've knowed Dave and Ramón long enough to know they never shot nobody in the back. All I'm sayin' is that *some* folks are goin' to wonder where a driftin' cowpoke got money enough to buy four ranches. Hell! I'm not about to write any letters, and I'm not about to arrest anybody. Now you get a good grip on your shirttail and hang onto it."

Jim pulled in a deep breath, rubbing a hand wearily across the back of his neck. "I'm sorry, Skeet," he said gruffly. "I'm sort of on edge today."

"Shore." Dorman laid a hand briefly on his shoulder, then cleared his throat. "What time did that shootin' come off?"

"Around nine o'clock, I reckon. I'm not shore."

Dorman nodded. "They'd have had time to get here, all right. The stage must have been held up about seven. How many men were there in the bunch?"

"Either three or four."

"Three," Dorman said with a positive inflection. "Same bunch, shore as the devil."

Dave flipped his hand in a contradictory gesture. "Why would Grant Talbot hold up the stage?"

Dorman looked at Dave carefully before answering. "I didn't say he did."

"Well, I'm sayin' it was Grant that done the shootin'," Dave said flatly.

"Maybe it was. Maybe it wasn't. You know, there's a hell of a lot of difference in what you think and what a lawman can prove. And you asked a mighty good question a while ago: Why *would* Grant hold up the stage?"

"Those tracks comin' up to this corral were awful plain," Eddie said idly, as if it were of no importance. "A kid could have followed 'em."

"Left a plain trail, did he?" Dave's voice took on a deadly edge. "Figured to kill Jim and get the rest of us framed for murder. Damn him!"

Jim abruptly turned his back on the group, leaning both arms over the neck of the horse and lifting a troubled gaze toward the northwest, where that stage robbery had taken place. He closed his mind to the argument still going on behind him, trying to gather in all the details of what had happened.

He hardly believed that Grant Talbot had been responsible for the robbery. Not that Grant was above framing the Five Drag men for robbery and murder, but last night Grant had been too busy committing murder himself. Of that Jim was still sure; and he was still sure that he was the one Grant had intended to kill, which would have made a frame-up unnecessary. The last vestige of fight would have gone out of Long John Dixon when he buried his son.

Something here didn't add up.

Jim turned slowly. "How do you figure, Skeet?"

"Hell!" Dorman spat disgustedly. "I been chasin' gun hands all over this damn country for the last three years. I couldn't figure too good to start with, and here lately I can't figure at all."

"Well, I got my part of the figurin' done," Jim said. "This stage robbery is your business."

"Jim—" Dorman started to lift a hand, then let it sag. "All right, boy, but for God's sake, be careful. Don't do anything that'd make me come after you."

"I won't." Jim straightened, ending the discussion. "You fellas better stay for supper."

"Sold," Dorman said promptly. "In fact, if you got an extra bed, I'll fall on it tonight."

"Say, Jim." Eddie shoved his hat to the back of his head, squinting at Jim with a keen speculation. "That offer of a job still open?"

"You betcha," Jim said quickly. He saw Dave's head jerk up, saw the old cowboy open his lips as if to speak; but he went on evenly, "You takin' me up on it?"

"Yeah, I believe I will. I been thinkin' it over." Eddie grinned and added dryly, "I didn't think at first that you'd live long enough to make it interestin', but I believe now you got possibilities."

"Eddie, I'll be damn glad to have you," Jim said feelingly. "There'll be plenty of grub and ammunition, but I can't guarantee how long the job'll last or what kind of pay you'll get."

"I'll take my pay in excitement," Eddie drawled with a grin.

"Is that all you're lookin' for?" Dave put in coldly.

The old cowboy, Jim saw, was challenging Eddie with a hard, bright stare. Eddie didn't answer, merely glancing at Dave with cool indifference before turning a questioning gaze to Jim.

Jim hid his sudden uneasiness behind a casual tone. "Dave, you and Ramón take Skeet in the house and let him get the weight off those poor creakin' boots. Eddie and I'll take care of these broncs."

Dave turned his head to give Jim a long, searching look that was heavy with warning. Then, without a word, he opened the gate, held it while Dorman and Ramón ambled through, and followed them toward the house, his boot heels hitting the ground with an angry cadence.

Jim pulled the saddle and bridle off Dorman's horse, hung them on the fence, and turned the animal in with the Five Drag remuda. Then he roped a chunky bay to keep in for a wrangle horse while Eddie turned all the others out into a small pasture above the corrals.

When the job was done, Jim said briefly, "Let's have a smoke."

They squatted on their spurs, their backs to the fence, and smoked in silence for several moments while Jim debated how best to voice his questions. Finally he said bluntly, "What's Dave got against you?"

Eddie shrugged. "Same thing everybody else has got against me, I reckon. I told you most folks figured I wasn't fit company."

"Yeah, I remember you did, and I told you then I didn't believe it. You and Dave haven't had any trouble, have you?"

"Not a bit of it. I like Dave, the old devil. Always have."

The subtle reserve Eddie had shown Jim in town seemed to be gone, and Jim felt more at ease under this straightforward sincerity. Eddie, he reflected, had always been wild and reckless. The son of a cowboy who'd been killed in a Bar X stampede down in the canyon, he had been a foot-loose, spur-jingling cow hand with a questionable reputation even before Jim left the country.

That reputation, however, had been based on his explosive willingness to fight, anywhere, any time; and Jim had always found him as loyal and lovable as a brother. In fact, he and Jim had backed each other to the limit in more than one Saturday-night fracas.

If his reputation now were based on no more ....

Jim turned for a casual inspection of him, his glance touching briefly on the second gun the cowboy was packing. "What you been doin' since you quit Ladder?"

"Nothin' much," Eddie admitted. "I drifted down into the minin' camps for a while. Learned enough about poker to keep myself in tobacco."

Jim grinned. "If I remember right, you didn't need to learn much in that department. How come you quit Ladder, Eddie?"

"I didn't. Grant fired me."

"What for?"

For the first time Eddie lifted his head and met Jim's gaze squarely. "I was showin' too much interest in Marilyn."

"Marilyn?" Jim echoed, stung.

"Yeah. I'd been takin' her to a few dances. Grant told me to lay off, but I didn't figure it was any of his business." His voice turned very dry. "He finally convinced me that it was."

Jim couldn't help the tight jealousy that sprang up in him, but he kept it out of his voice. "Did he whip you?"

"Shore, he whipped me," Eddie said frankly. "I ain't no fighter with my fists, not when a guy's that big, anyhow. He ran me off the range, saw to it that nobody'd hire me."

"How could he do that?" Jim demanded.

Again Eddie looked at him squarely. "He claimed I was rustlin' cattle."

Eddie didn't put it into words, but it was there in his eyes, and Jim dropped his head. It hadn't been just Marilyn. It had been partly the fact that Eddie Worthington was a friend of Jim Dixon's, the man Grant couldn't get his hands on.

"Since then," Eddie finished, "I been just kinda hangin' around, waitin' for a chance to get even."

"And that's the main reason you took this job, to get a crack at Ladder?"

"Main reason, yeah." A sudden, reckless grin lit Eddie's face. "Hell, cowboy. I just plain like a good fight, and you're shore headed for one!"

Jim abruptly stood up, flipping his cigarette away and pulling in a breath that swelled his chest. "Eddie, I appreciate your tellin' me all this," he said deliberately, "and the deal still goes. I don't give a damn about your reputation as long as you're square with Five Drag."

Eddie pushed slowly to his feet, his eyes once more burning with that queer, intense light. "You're the only pard I ever had, Jim."

Jim stuck out his hand but he couldn't force a grin, and they turned toward the house in uncomfortable silence. Try as he would, Jim couldn't quell the hot resentment that flooded through him every time he thought of Eddie's being in love with Marilyn; and he wondered what effect that would have on their friendship. When they had been pards before, they had not been in love with the same woman.

Stubbornly, he shoved the thought out of his mind. Eddie was a good man to have along in a fight, and Five Drag needed him. As far as Marilyn was concerned, she had made it plain that she was no longer any of Jim Dixon's business.

CHAPTER SIX

JIM was up at three o'clock the next morning. He got the fire going, the coffee on, and the biscuits mixed before stepping out the back door and letting out a yell that was guaranteed to waken anybody within half a mile. Then he cut thick steaks off the quarter of beef that had been hung on the back porch and had the meat frying by the time Skeet, Dave, and Ramón clumped into the kitchen.

"Damn me," Skeet said querulously. "A man can shore spend a night awful quick in this camp."

"What do you want?" Dave retorted. "The world with a fence around it and hell throwed in for a calf pasture?"

The old cowboy's eyes, Jim noted, were as keen as a couple of well-whetted knives. Ramón, too, had a sparkle in his black eyes that was not all due to the prospect of a fight with Ladder. These two old brush-poppers had missed the roundup.

"Eddie wranglin'?" Jim asked.

"Yeah," Dave said, and Jim could detect no rancor in his voice.

The men did not eat hurriedly, but they tended to business, dispensing with conversation while they filled their stomachs against whatever the day might bring. Jim was the first one through. He refilled the coffee cups and rolled a cigarette, smoking in silence until Skeet shoved his plate back with a satisfied sigh.

"One of those fellas," Jim said then, "Bell I think it was, said Grant had a big herd bunched. How come? He gatherin' beef in the spring, too?"

"Yeah," Skeet answered idly. "He's been shippin' twice a year. The way things have been here lately, steaks are safer in the fryin' pan than they are on the hoof."

"Brady shippin' twice a year, too?"

"No, he's just been shippin' in the fall; but he holds his stuff out of the roundup and takes it back down in the canyon."

Jim said, "He figures it's safe enough on the hoof, which means that safety's got nothin' to do with Grant shippin' in the spring."

Skeet's eyes took on a glint of humor, but it was Eddie who answered.

"When a man's cows all have triplets," he drawled, "he's got to thin his herd more often."

"Course, you know," Skeet said with elaborate gravity, "Grant buys a lot of young stuff. At least," he added, the humor gone out of his eyes, "I haven't been able to catch him gettin' it any other way."

"Is he holdin' a stray herd?" Jim asked.

"If he is," Dave spoke up bluntly, "it's just because he's waitin' for the calves to get big enough to wean."

Jim finished his coffee and stood up. "Well, I got a hunch he's holdin' *our* stuff. Anyhow, we'll go see."

He dumped his dishes in the wreck pan and led the way to the corral, hunching his shoulders against the chill night air. The horses, too, felt the briskness of the night and presented a snorting, dodging mass that made the roping of any one of them a form of the highest art. Jim snared Cappy and led him out to the saddle shed.

With all five horses finally saddled and ready to go, Jim turned to Dorman and clamped a hand on his shoulder. "Come out and see us again, Skeet."

"I ain't gone home yet," Skeet said gruffly. "I haven't sat in on a good roundup for a right smart spell, don't you know it?"

"If you sit in on this one—" Jim began.

"Don't object to me trailin' along, do you?" Skeet interrupted.

"Skeet, you know I don't, but you may be linin' yourself up with the short side of a mighty risky argument."

Skeet swung into his saddle. "Anybody wants to take a shot at me," he grunted, "better make the first one count. And like I said, I ain't worked cattle since the Pinal Mountains was a hole in the ground. You comin'?"

The sky was lighting to the east when Jim lifted his hand and stopped his riders at the edge of the last thick stand of mesquite bordering the *ciénaga* holding grounds. The ride down in the crisp predawn air, with the familiar creak of leather and the jingle of spurs and bit chains, had tended to ease the tension under which he had been laboring, and he felt ready for anything.

Two campfires burned out on the flat, one to the southwest of the water hole and one to the north of it, nearer the canyon. Brady, evidently, was using his own wagon. Beyond this second fire, Jim could see the dark bulk of a herd—the cattle Brady would be shoving down into the canyon when the roundup was over.

"Reckon we'll see Brady first," Jim said briefly, and led the way at a walk toward the Bar X wagon.

Saddled horses stood around the camp, reins dragging, while the cowboys sat or knelt near the fire, eating a hurried breakfast. They looked up, startled, as the Five Drag men rode in. Then Milt Brady set his plate on a rock and stepped forward, his sun-reddened face breaking into a grin as he extended his hand.

"Heard you were back, Jim. Good to see you."

"Thanks, Milt," Jim replied, taking the hand without dismounting. He remembered Brady as a bluff, kindly man who liked to avoid trouble but who was as straight as a die. He wondered whether the rancher had changed.

Brady nodded at the other riders, then asked matter-of-factly, "You boys joinin' the roundup?"

Jim grinned. "You don't believe it, do you, Milt?"

"Well—" Brady looked at the ground and kicked half-heart-edly at a rock. "You sure could as far as I'm concerned."

"You willing to back my play?" Jim asked bluntly.

Slowly the rancher shook his head. "I can't afford to, Jim."

"You shore you can afford not to? You know which way Ladder'll be movin' next if they manage to take over Five Drag!"

Again Brady shook his head. "Don't believe Grant will ever bother me if I mind my own business, which I'm sure aimin' to do."

Jim lifted his glance to the cowboys, who had stopped eating to listen. Their dark, still faces told him nothing. He looked back at Brady and asked roughly, "What about this morning? You gonna mind your own business then, too?

A slow grin twisted Brady's lips as he looked up. "Still got your temper, I see," he drawled, his tone utterly friendly. "The answer's yes, Jim. You can count the Bar X out of any trouble that starts."

Jim pulled in a deep breath and grinned back, unable to stay sore at this easygoing old-timer. "Reckon that'll have to do. Is Grant holdin' a stray herd?"

"No-o-o," Brady answered, his eyes sparkling. "He's holdin' your stuff with his beef herd."

For a moment Jim remained quiet, his arms resting on his saddle horn, searching the face of the canyon rancher for every-thing it had to tell him. Then he straightened, lifted one hand in salute, and reined out of camp.

He made a wide circle around the Ladder wagon, riding at an easy jog, and headed for the big herd that was grazing beyond it. Skeet rode beside him, stirrup to stirrup, while Eddie, Dave, and Ramón brought up the rear of the compact little group.

The murkiness of dawn was lifting rapidly now, and Jim could plainly see the furor in the Ladder camp when he and his men were discovered. Almost immediately, more than a dozen riders swirled out of the camp and came on at a dead run, Grant

Talbot half a length in the lead and quirting his horse at every stride.

Jim did not increase his pace. He glanced again at the herd, saw the two riders on guard loping around it to intercept him. Then, almost lazily, he pulled his .30-30 out of the scabbard and levered a shell into the barrel, holding the gun in his right hand with the stock caught under his forearm and the barrel slightly lifted, ready to snap down on any target. Behind him he heard two other rifles receive their deadly charges and knew that Eddie would rely on his two handguns. Skeet Dorman shifted in the saddle, straightening his right leg and resting his hand idly on his hip.

Jim turned his narrowed gaze back to Grant, aware that his breathing was growing ragged, although he had never felt cooler in his life. The promise he had made his dad was like a strong hand on his arm, steadying him, holding his hatred in tight restraint.

Fifty feet from the edge of the herd he pulled up, swinging Cappy directly to face the Ladder outfit as Grant pulled his horse to a plunging halt and his men spread out to either side of him. Grant's eyes, above the stubble of dirty yellow beard on his face, were glittering like stars on a frosty night.

"What the hell do you want?" he demanded stridently.

"My cattle," Jim said.

Grant made a furious gesture with his left hand. "No rustler outfit is cuttin' my herd!"

"Maybe not," Jim drawled coolly, "but *I'm* cuttin' it, and I'm startin' right now. Want to stop me?"

Grant hesitated, flashing a wicked glance at Skeet. "You on their side in this?"

"Generally," Skeet said, without inflection, "I'm on the side of law and order. You know of any law says a man can't get his own cattle out of a roundup?"

Grant pulled in a hissing breath, turning his eyes back to Jim and flicking a coldly calculating glance at the rifle in Jim's hand.

Jim's thumb on the hammer tightened until his knuckle turned white. He was aware that Rennick, on Grant's left, had his hands played above his gun while the other men had their narrowed eyes on Grant, awaiting only the signal to start.

Jim kept his own eyes glued to Grant as he said softly, "The first one goes right through your flapjacks, cowboy."

Slowly Grant settled in his saddle and laid his right hand carefully over his saddle horn. "All right," he said through his teeth. "Take your damn cattle. Get 'em off my range and keep 'em off it!"

Without for a moment relaxing his guard, Jim said, "Dave, you and Eddie run 'em out. Ramón, hold 'em."

The work went swiftly in spite of the size of the herd, since Talbot had held only beef in his own brand, and the cows and calves were all Jim's. Jim rested the butt of the rifle against his thigh, his manner cool and almost careless; but his eyes grew strained and his breathing became gradually tighter. He could see the fury mounting in Grant as the latter watched the cattle being run out of the herd.

"You reppin' for Bell and Lathrop?" Grant demanded.

"I'm cuttin' their stuff," Jim replied, and let it go at that.

Grant swore viciously but made no move to interfere. Skeet Dorman hadn't moved a muscle since he reined to a halt beside Jim, his hand still resting on his hip; but Jim could feel the menacing presence of the man and knew that Ladder could feel it even more.

Then Eddie pulled up beside him and said quietly, "She's clean, Jim."

Jim could hear Dave and Ramón getting the herd started, and he waited until their subsiding yells told him the cattle were moving out. Then he said evenly, "I'm not reppin' for Bell and Lathrop, no. I bought 'em out, along with Holmes and Smith."

"Bought 'em out?" Grant echoed, his voice streaking up to a yell.

"Yeah. Those four places belong to Five Drag now, and you and your men stay off of 'em."

For a second Grant hung poised while a red wave washed up his neck and turned to a purplish hue under his beard. His whole right arm began to quiver.

"Look out, Talbot!" Skeet rang out sharply.

Grant caught himself, but Rennick made a lightning-swift stab for his gun. Jim didn't hesitate for an instant. He snapped the barrel of his rifle down and fired. He saw the slug take Rennick full in the chest, stopping him cold; and he swung the leveled rifle in a slow arc across the other men, at the same time jerking up a tight rein on the quivering Cappy.

The swift deadliness of his action had stunned the Ladder outfit into immobility. Not a man stirred as Rennick folded slowly over his saddle horn and slid down his horse's shoulder, his half-drawn gun tipping out of the holster as he fell. The thud of his body was jarringly loud in the shocked silence.

Jim kept his rifle leveled, ready, as he backed his horse slowly away from the group, Skeet and Eddie moving with him. Not until they were a hundred feet away did they whirl their horses and jump them into a run. Jim saw then that Dave was on the ground behind his horse, his rifle cradled across his saddle as he covered their retreat.

They put a quick half mile behind them, then saw that the Ladder outfit was moving slowly back toward the wagon. Skeet wiped a sleeve across his glistening jaw.

"For God's sake, Jim," he complained. "Did you have to pick a time like that to rub it into him about those places you bought? Why didn't you waltz over and pull his whiskers while you were at it?"

Eddie laughed joyously. "Kinda provoked him, didn't it? To think he softened those guys up for Jim's pocketbook!"

Jim didn't answer, still gripped as he was by an icy passion. He shoved the rifle back into the scabbard, wiped his sweating hands on his shirt. Then he rolled a cigarette and felt the smoke gradually ease the cramp of his tautened nerves.

They took the cattle to the Lazy L, which had a good set of corrals although the adobe house and few outbuildings looked barren and dilapidated in the early-morning sun. Lathrop and his family had already moved out, taking only their personal belongings, a wagon, and one team of horses.

While the branding irons were heating, Jim sat back against the fence and once more looked over the herd he had penned. There were not over two hundred cows in the bunch, and most of them were Five Drag's. There were a few wearing the Bell brand and the Lazy L, but Jim saw only one Box S and no JH's. And there was not a yearling or two-year-old in any of the five brands.

"Not as many as I figured," he said, turning a challenging glance to Skeet, who had sat down next to him. "And not as many as there ought to be."

"Granted," Skeet said shortly. "Somebody's been takin' not only all the calves but part of the cows."

"Of course," Jim said with mild sarcasm, "this isn't all of 'em. You notice there isn't a baby calf in this bunch. Grant was holdin' only the big calves, the ones that would be weaners before fall."

"Yeah," Dave put in, in a taunting drawl, "and holdin' 'em with his beef herd, at that!"

"You fellers don't need to tell me," Skeet said flatly. "I got eyes, damnit all to hell, but what I ain't got is evidence. Knowin' what a man intends to do—or even knowin' what he's done—and catchin' him at it is two different things. Besides, boys—" Skeet hesitated, scratching the back of his head vigorously. "Grant's been crowdin' awful hard. He wants this whole valley, especially Five Drag, because of the feed and water you got."

"And other reasons," Jim said curtly.

"And other reasons," Skeet acknowledged. "I don't doubt for a minute that he's been brandin' calves he knew weren't his. But, honestly, I don't believe he's been runnin' off branded stuff."

"Then who's doin' it?" Jim demanded.

"God, Jim, it might be anybody," Skeet said, spreading his hands in a helpless gesture. "Who's been robbin' these stages? I can't believe Ladder's doin' that, either."

Eddie looked up with a hard, squinted gaze. "I could believe Grant Talbot'd do anything," he said deliberately. "He's a hog for power *and* money."

"Maybe," Skeet conceded, "but I'm gonna have to catch him at it 'fore I say it out loud."

Jim rolled a cigarette in thoughtful silence, recalling what his dad had said about the riffraff that had been drifting into the country. He had said they left Ladder alone because the outfit was too powerful to buck. Jim had doubted the statement then, and his doubts were growing apace. He was more inclined to agree with Eddie than with Skeet, but concrete evidence was what they all lacked.

"What I'd like to know," Skeet said, "is whether you bullheaded fire-eaters are gonna keep on cuttin' that roundup."

Jim grinned broadly and shook his head. "My curiosity's satisfied. I just kinda wanted to check up on things."

"*And* show Grant you could do it," Skeet said keenly.

"Yeah," Jim admitted, his grin turning rueful. "I kinda enjoyed it, but the next time might not be so funny. He may not hold any more of 'em, anyway."

"Even if he does," Dave drawled, with a significant look at Jim, "a lot can happen between now and fall. Grant ain't got *any* shippin' done yet!"

Jim abruptly stood up. "Which end of this cattle-workin' business," he asked Skeet, "are you the most anxious to brush up on?"

"Well—" Skeet grunted as he climbed to his feet, "I can't rope and I'm too fat to flank 'em, but I shore got weight enough to hold 'em down after somebody else throws 'em."

"Which I got a hunch," Eddie said dryly, "is goin' to be my job. Drag 'em out, somebody. I'm shore feelin' tough."

Jim glanced quickly at Dave; but if the old cowboy approved of Eddie's willingness to take on the hardest job in the roundup, he gave no sign of it. Nevertheless, Jim felt sure that such an attitude was bound to improve the relationship between the two men, and he gave Eddie a grateful slap on the back as he strode past him toward the fire.

Dave did the roping and Jim did the branding, running the Five Drag on all the calves regardless of the parent brand. Skeet helped Eddie hold them down while Ramón wielded a pocket knife, putting a dexterous swallow-fork in the left ear and an underbit in the right.

The five men very quickly adjusted themselves into a well-co-ordinated team that kept the calves bawling, the dust flying, and the sweat rolling. It was late in the afternoon when Jim straightened up from the last calf, mopping his face with a dusty sleeve and grinning at the red-faced deputy sheriff, who was holding his back with both hands.

"First honest day's work you've done for ninety years," he accused.

"I've lost ten pounds," Skeet panted, "and I ain't even got strength enough to hunt for 'em."

"Well, Skeet, I shore appreciate the help. In fact," Jim added frankly, "I appreciate the whole day."

"All I ask," Skeet retorted, "is that you come to my funeral. I don't believe I'll last till mornin'."

They drove the cattle up out of the flat and pointed them toward the creek above the Bell place before letting them go. Jim pulled up on the crest of a low, open ridge and slid sideways in the saddle as he let his gaze wander over the vast country that was now his, relishing a satisfaction that was keen even though grim.

He knew there would be no chance in the immediate future to do anything with the small ranches, but the land was there and it would keep. Someday those scattered parcels would be welded into one beautiful ranch—if he could hold them and stay alive.

He twisted in the saddle, running a speculative eye over the high ridge that separated Five Drag from the Smith place, then swinging back to look at the sharp spur of the Pinals that reached out toward the valley beyond the Bell place. The canyon in which Five Drag was situated had widened out here, its floor broken by sandy washes and low, mesquite-covered ridges.

Then he looked at the four men who were smoking in weary silence and grinned. "You fellers like to dig postholes?" he inquired mildly.

"Fire me," Skeet blurted. "Please!"

"Postholes?" Dave said blankly. "What for do you want any postholes?"

'Did you notice Grant's *cienaga* this morning?" Jim asked.

"Shore. It's awful low. Be dry in less than a month."

"Deep Creek'll be dryin' up, too, which means that Grant will be drivin' up through here again to get at our spring. But if we'd build a drift fence ..." Jim let a swing of his arm finish the sentence.

Eddie took one swift look and then spoke dismally, with a cowpuncher's natural hatred not only of fences but of footwork. "Five miles, at least. God help me!"

Skeet, Dave and Ramón spent several moments swinging their heads back and forth, looking from the ridge to the spur and back again, before Skeet spoke excitedly.

"By golly, Jim, it'll work!"

"Shore, it'll work," Dave corroborated, as if the idea had been his in the first place. "Grass is pretty short up here, but there'll be plenty mesquite beans to take care of our stuff, and our grass'll come back if Ladder keeps off of it."

"The job," Jim said, "is as good as done. After we get the fence up, we'll work the mountain for strays and mavericks."

"By God!" Dave breathed, his eyes suddenly gleaming. "We're goin' back into the cow business!"

"And I'm goin' to town and get a drink," Eddie said flatly. "I'll shore need one if I'm goin' to build fence. You ridin' in, Skeet?"

"Yeah."

"I'll go with you," Jim said. "I could use a beer myself."

Dave and Ramón declined to go, and the men split up. Little was said on the way to town. Skeet, evidently, was too tired to talk, and Jim was too busy with his plans for the future. He felt a grim elation over the realization that he had hit Grant a double blow today, and this was just the beginning.

Both his thoughts and his elation were rudely interrupted, however, when Eddie pulled up a short distance from town.

"I reckon," the cowboy drawled with a tight grin, "that with most of the Ladder outfit out on roundup, this is a good time for me to see my girl. I'll see you gents later."

Jim felt a leap of instant, unreasoning anger, but he only said, with gruff warning, "Keep your eyes peeled."

"Shore. Grant won't get his hands on me a second time."

Jim kept his eyes glued stonily to the ground ahead of him as Eddie reined aside and spurred into a lope toward the Ladder headquarters.

CHAPTER SEVEN

B Y THE time he reached town, Jim had himself in hand, having once more shoved his feeling for Marilyn down into some hidden pocket in his make-up. He offered to buy Skeet a drink in appreciation of the day's work, but the deputy declined.

As Skeet rode on down the street, Jim reined in at Miller's store, remembering that he owed someone else an expression of gratitude. Donna was not in sight, but the old Judge leaned against the tobacco counter, his gray hair, as usual, rumpled and unruly.

"Howdy, Jim," he said laconically.

"Howdy, Judge. How's everything goin'?"

"All right with me."

There was an inflection in his voice that caused Jim to look at him sharply; but the Judge was looking at the floor, his head bent as he rubbed reflectively behind one ear. Jim sauntered over to the counter and leaned against it as he rolled a cigarette, slightly uneasy.

"I hear," the Judge said finally, without inflection, "that you been buyin' ranches."

"Yeah? Where'd you hear that?"

"Ace and Bennett came in a while ago."

Jim didn't know Ace, but he remembered Bennett, a dark-faced, hard-eyed man who'd been on the Ladder payroll for years. He remembered, in fact, having seen the man at the *ciénaga* that morning. He lit his cigarette, studying the Judge's face over the match and seeing a restraint that had not been there the day before.

"So Ace and Bennett been totin' the news around, eh?" he drawled. "What else did they have to say?"

"About Rennick, of course." The Judge looked at Jim and looked away again. "Don't suppose you had to pay too much for those four places, did you?"

Jim straightened and gave the old storekeeper a hard, straight glance. "I paid a thousand bucks apiece for 'em," he said deliberately, "and I got a little left. Just how much did the express company lose in that stage robbery, anyhow?"

The Judge drew back, pulling in a sharp breath as his face turned red. "Now, take it easy, Jim," he said in alarm. "I didn't say you had anything to do with that robbery."

"But Ace and Bennett said it, and you got half a notion to believe 'em. Well, hop to it, if you feel that way." Jim took an angry pull at his cigarette. Skeet had said folks would wonder, but it had never occurred to Jim that "folks" might include the Millers. Then he saw the distress on the Judge's face, and he softened his tone a little. "Grant shore didn't waste any time startin' his rumors, did he?"

"No, he—Jim, you took me wrong. I was just curious as to what you'd have to say, because—well—"

He finished with a vague gesture, but Jim understood it and his anger washed out. The Judge was thinking about his daughter, in love with a man who was a mighty logical suspect for robbery and murder.

"Why don't you pull out while you can, Jim? You're bucking something you can't lick!"

"Maybe." Jim glanced out the door toward the Mescal saloon, where three saddled horses dozed at the hitch rack. "Ace and Bennett?"

"They're over there."

"Well, I reckon I'll go see if they got guts enough to tell *me* I'm a stage robber."

He dropped his cigarette and stepped on it, pulling his hat down hard as he turned toward the door. As he stalked outside, he nearly collided with Donna, who was reaching for the door-knob while looking back over her shoulder at Cappy. Jim grabbed her outstretched hand and said, "Whoa."

Donna jerked her head around with a gasp, then was instantly laughing and blushing at the same time. She withdrew her hand, but the eager sparkle remained in her eyes.

"I saw your horse," she admitted, "and thought I better amble down to see if you were still all right."

"You wouldn't amble right over the top of a fella, would you?"

"Well, if he got in my way when I was in a hurry." She laughed again. "How's everything?"

"Pickin' up," Jim said with a grin. Her warm, friendly presence and her obvious loyalty gave him a stirring lift, and he found himself looking at her with a new appreciation. No wild rumors would find lodgment in her dark, pretty head. "Say," he said suddenly, "I believe I owe you some thanks."

"What for?"

"That cake. It's shore good."

His statement startled her. "How'd you know I made that?" she demanded.

"I don't know," he grinned. "Just looked like you, sort of."

"Well, heavens," she murmured. "I don't know whether that's a compliment or not."

"Well, it shore is."

She hesitated, searching his face and evidently finding something that reassured her. Her eyes took on a mischievous glint. "There's a dance coming up in three or four weeks."

"Oh, yeah?" Jim felt a quick pang at the memory of other dances in this town, but he didn't let it interfere. "Reckon I'll have to be on hand for that."

"I figured you'd want to know about it," she said, striving to speak matter-of-factly when she had become confused by her own audacity.

"You betcha." Jim lifted his head at the sound of sudden loud voices over in the Mescal, followed by the crash of a table or chair to the floor. He glanced back at Donna and grinned at the anxiety that had sprung into her eyes. "I'll be at the dance," he assured her pointedly. "See you later, Donna."

He touched his hat brim to her, then turned and and stepped off the walk, striding leisurely across the street toward the saddle and harness shop. He didn't enter it, however, but cut into a passageway between it and the feed store and came in behind the Mescal. Soundlessly he let himself in the back door and crossed the small room that was used for storage purposes, hearing the run of angry voices out front. In the door to the main room he momentarily pulled up.

The Mescal was not large, never very well lighted, and never very clean. A badly scuffed bar stretched halfway down the south side of the room to Jim's left, while the right side and the rear were cluttered with tables and chairs.

There were only four men in the place—the slight, gray-haired bartender who stood rooted with apprehension, and three cowboys planted on widespread legs near an overturned table. Jim recognized Bennett and took a quick, calculating look at Ace, a medium-sized man with a blunt jaw and pale blue eyes that held a frosty glint. Facing them defiantly was a dark, slender cowboy who couldn't have been more than twenty-one.

"You're not runnin' this town," he said angrily, "and you're not runnin' the country."

"But we're runnin' rustlers out of it," Ace replied in a cold drawl. "You don't seem to have guts enough to throw a gun, so we'll just give your friends somethin' to think about. Hold him, Bennett."

As Bennett stepped forward, the young cowboy lunged at him, landing a glancing blow on Bennett's jaw before Ace grabbed him from behind. There was a short, vicious struggle during which Jim stepped through the doorway and moved warily through the scattered tables. The men were too busy to see his approach; and he was directly behind Ace when that individual stepped back, deliberately knotting his right fist while Bennett wrenched the struggling cowboy's arms behind him and held him helpless.

As Ace swung his arm back to deliver the blow, Jim grabbed his shoulder and spun him around. He had a fleeting glimpse of the startled expression on the man's face. Then he smashed his right fist into the middle of that face with every ounce of his weight behind it.

He felt his knuckles grind on bone, and he felt some of that bone give way and shatter. Ace's head snapped back, and his arms flew up as he crashed backward into the bar and caromed off it, tangling his spurs in the brass railing and landing on his side with a jar that shook the whole building.

Jim caught his balance, bracing himself on stiff legs as he swung to face Bennett. The man was in the act of giving the young cowboy a shove that sent him sprawling. Then he twisted back, starting to reach for his gun, but his hand froze in mid-air as he recognized Jim.

"Go ahead," Jim said, as cold as ice. "Maybe Rennick's lonesome."

With infinite care, Bennett lifted his hands as high as his shoulders. "He can stay lonesome for all of me," he said, his voice even in spite of the pallor that had spread over his face.

The cowboy had scrambled to his feet but he stopped short, staring. Ace was on his hands and knees, swinging his head slowly from side to side while the blood poured from his broken nose in a steady stream.

Slowly Jim straightened, placing his hands on his hips as he eyed Bennett with open contempt. "I came over here to see if you had nerve enough to call me a thief to my face, but I see you haven't. You're a liar, Bennett, and you know it."

"I was just—"

"Just repeatin' what Grant told you to say, huh? You slinkin', yellow-bellied pup! Take your little playmate and get out of here."

Bennett seemed glad enough to go. He pulled the groggy Ace to his feet and, balancing him precariously, guided him out through the swinging doors. Jim didn't move until he heard the two men riding out of town. Then he turned to the cowboy.

"How about a drink?"

The cowboy pulled in a deep breath and then grinned, a flashing of white teeth that was irresistible. "Let me buy you one," he countered. He stepped forward, extending his hand. "My name's Ryan. Tommy Ryan. And somethin' tells me you're Jim Dixon."

Afterward, as they leaned against the bar smoking, Tommy looked up with an unfathomable light in his dark eyes. "I sure do thank you," he said slowly. "Most folks wouldn't have figured I was worth helpin'."

"I enjoyed myself," Jim replied honestly, then voiced a question he'd been mulling over. "You by any chance lookin' for a job?"

Tommy hesitated. "Did you hear what Ace called me?"

"Yeah, I heard him," Jim drawled, "but that doesn't mean much. That Ladder outfit's kinda free and easy with their name-callin'. They got me entered in their little book as a stage robber."

"Well—" Tommy grinned. "I hate like hell to run, and it's a cinch I can't lick 'em by myself."

"You're hired," Jim said, satisfied with the deal. "Let's go home."

It was late in the evening when Eddie got back to the ranch. Jim was in the kitchen alone, trying to figure out how much wire he would need for his fence, when the cowboy strode in, his spurs trailing across the floor with a pleasant-sounding jingle.

"How's chances for a handout?" he asked gaily. "I'm shore one starved cowpuncher."

"Meat and beans on the back of the stove," Jim answered, and kept his eyes on the figures in front of him, although he was no longer seeing them. Eddie's cheerful manner stung him, suggesting as it did that his visit with Marilyn had been highly satisfactory.

Jim continued staring at the paper while Eddie filled his plate and brought it to the table. Then he tossed his pencil aside and tipped his chair back against the wall, rolling a cigarette while he sorted out the questions he had to ask.

"Marilyn knew I was goin' to cut that herd," he said finally, "but I don't believe she told Grant. She say anything about it?"

"A little."

"What?" Jim prompted, as Eddie hesitated.

"Well, she said if she'd known you were actually goin' through with it, she'd have warned Grant you were comin'." He hesitated again, then went on with obvious reluctance. "She seemed to figure maybe it was her fault Rennick got killed."

"Because she didn't warn 'em?"

"Yeah."

"How does she figure that? Rennick was free, white, and old enough to know what he was doin'."

"Yeah, but—"

"But what?" Jim demanded, as Eddie once more paused.

Eddie set his fork down carefully and looked up, his eyes deep and inscrutable in the flickering lamplight. "She said if Rennick had had time to think, he'd have known he didn't have a chance against you."

Jim turned cold all over. He didn't want to ask the question because he knew he wasn't going to like the answer, but his tight jealousy wouldn't let him back up. "Just what does she think I am, anyway?"

"A wanton killer."

Eddie dropped the words out slowly, and each one of them cut into Jim like a dull knife. He looked down at his cigarette, suddenly aware that his breathing was shallow, inadequate; but he wouldn't admit his weakness by changing the rhythm of it.

A strained silence fell between them; and when Eddie spoke again, his voice had changed subtly.

"What do you care what she thinks, Jim?"

"I don't," Jim said shortly.

"You used to like her pretty well, didn't you?"

Jim glanced up but looked quickly back at his cigarette, sensing the suspicion that had prompted the question. "We were just kids then," he said gruffly.

"Shore," Eddie acknowledged. "Four years is a long time, but some folks don't change."

"And some folks *do* change!" Jim let his chair legs drop back to the floor and picked up the paper on which he had been making his calculations. "It's a good thing," he said in a disarming drawl, "that you got your gallivantin' done tonight, 'cause startin' tomorrow, cowboy, you're goin' to be plumb up to your ears in postholes."

For a long moment Eddie eyed him searchingly but finally grinned and reached for his fork. "Like a damn gopher," he said in disgust. "If we got to use a shovel, anyway, I believe it'd be cheaper just to dig a few more graves."

Jim stabbed a fiery glance at him, but the cowboy had turned his attention back to his belated meal, apparently unaware that his remark had rubbed an open sore; apparently, also, satisfied that the affair between Jim and Marilyn was definitely a thing of the past.

Jim smothered a curse, running a hand through his rumpled black hair as he stared once more at the figures he had written. He still couldn't see them.

At dawn the next morning, Jim got Ramón started to Wilson after the wire, then strode to the corrals, where the other men had their horses already saddled and were gathering up the tools they would need for the job. Shovels, axes, crowbars that would be needed on hard, rocky ground. As Jim got the rope off his saddle and started toward the horse corral, Tommy Ryan approached him hesitantly.

"Say, Jim, I didn't say nothin' about it last night 'cause I wasn't sure, but I been thinkin'."

"What about?"

"This business." Tommy waved his hand in a gesture that included the whole range. "You're takin' on a pretty good-sized job, and I wondered if you needed more help."

"I'll take all the help I can get," Jim said bluntly, wondering what lay behind the cowboy's embarrassment. "You know anybody lookin' for a job? This kind of a job?" he added, waving his own hand in a gesture that included everything Tommy had indicated.

"Yeah. I got a pard camped over here a ways." Tommy jerked his head toward Devil's Pass. "Slim Ellers. He ain't afraid to work, and he's an awful good man to have along in a fight, I'll tell you that."

"Then what weren't you sure of last night?"

Tommy flushed, but he looked at Jim squarely. "His reputation ain't no better'n mine is," he said evenly, "but he don't like Grant Talbot no better than I do, either."

"Go get him,' Jim said without hesitation. "And, Tommy, I don't mind tellin' you, I don't give a damn what you might have done anywhere else. It's what you do here on Five Drag that'll count with me."

Slowly Tommy straightened, unconsciously squaring his shoulders. Then his white teeth flashed in a grin. "Yessir!" he said, and turned eagerly toward his horse.

"We'll be down here about four miles, next to that high ridge," Jim called after him. "You can find us."

Jim went on into the horse corral, feeling a queer tingle of pleasure. It had been a long time, he judged, since anyone had honored Tommy Ryan by trusting him. The boy might have earned his shady reputation, but he still had decency enough to be ashamed of it; and Jim had a hunch that he could be made into a good worker.

During the next few days he proved, at least, that he was a good worker, willing and capable; and Jim missed no chance to praise or encourage him. The result was that Tommy's grin flashed every time Jim came within grinning distance. Slim Ellers, a lanky, towheaded, blueeyed cowboy, also made a good hand, and the fence line moved across the canyon with surprising speed.

When Ramón returned with the wire, Jim split the crew into three teams. He gave Dave and the Yaqui the job of getting posts, since it would give the old cowboys a chance to be in the saddle part of the time, snaking the posts in at the end of their ropes. Slim and Tommy dug the holes and set the posts while Eddie and Jim handled the wire, a job that kept not only their shirts but also their tempers and vocabularies ragged.

"My God!" Eddie said once, as he stopped for breath. "And to think I hired out to fight!"

"You'll get your chance to fight," Jim retorted grimly. "Wait'll Grant rams his nose into this fence."

They didn't attempt to set any posts in the bottom of the dry sandy washes, since they would wash out at the first heavy rain, anyway. In these spots they fastened light stays to the wires to keep them separated, then hung rocks on the bottom of the fence to hold it near the ground. They made two gates, one due east of the Lazy L and one on the creek near the Bell place.

They finished the job in a little less than two weeks. Then, while Dave and Ramón went after cattle and the other three men patrolled the fence, Jim saddled Cappy and jogged down toward the flat to do a little scouting. About halfway between the new fence and the Lazy L, he rode into a wide, shallow depression that was rutted and pockmarked from the hoofs of cattle. Jim pulled up abruptly, stung by a new idea.

Rain water had evidently collected here, for a short time at least. The depression lay at the foot of a long, gentle slope that would drain a lot of country; and Jim saw that by deepening the depression a little and piling the dirt into a dam on the lower side, he could form a tank that would hold the water for months.

"More footwork," he told Cappy, "but it'd give us water of our own down here on the flat. We'll do it."

He skirted the Lazy L and, riding warily, headed for the *ciénaga*. He felt sure the roundup on the flats had been completed, but he didn't care to meet any strange riders—unless he could be sure of seeing them first. The water hole, he found, was so nearly dry that cattle stood around it by the hundreds, bawling incessantly.

"That's the herd," he muttered grimly, "that we're goin' to collect against our fence; and we're goin' to collect 'em in the next day or two."

There was not a rider in sight as Jim turned away and headed out toward the JH for a brief inspection of his newly acquired property. The range, he found, was not in bad shape, particularly on the ridges that sloped down from the mountain; but the cattle using it were predominantly Ladder. The fact angered him, but there was nothing he could do about it for the time being.

The country grew rougher as he neared the JH, which was located back next to the mountain in a brushy, rugged canyon. As Jim reined out of the last steep wash below the ranch, he saw instantly the dust cloud hanging in the air and heard the muffled bawling of a cow. He jerked Cappy to a halt, hesitating only a moment before whirling the horse and jumping back into the wash.

He turned downcountry, covering a swift quarter of a mile before again climbing out of the wash. Taking advantage of the brushy cover, he crossed the floor of the canyon, circled around behind a high knoll that would command a good view, and turned Cappy up the steep ascent. Just short of the top, he dismounted and left his horse tied in the shelter of a clump of oak.

Cautiously, he made his way on up the knoll, where a cluster of huge granite boulders and a few scraggly trees provided good cover. He slipped around the rocks, saw a figure in the trees not fifteen feet away, and dropped to one knee, flashing a hand to his gun. Then his whole body turned rigid as he saw the long, fair hair that tumbled from under the brown hat.

Marilyn had her back to him, holding to the trunk of a tree as she peered off up the canyon. Soundlessly, Jim stepped out of the rocks and strode up behind her, stopping, hands on hips, only a few feet away.

"You the outpost?" he asked then, bitingly.

Marilyn whirled with a gasp, both hands thrown back around the tree behind her. For a second she stared, her eyes wide open. Then she let her breath out carefully and as carefully erased all expression from her face.

"Any law against looking at the country?" she countered. "Or do you charge for it?"

"Who's down there?"

"Down where?"

Jim jerked his head at the canyon. "Those cattle aren't roundin' themselves up, and I'm the only Five Drag man out here. Who is it?"

Marilyn's glance wavered. "Ace and Bennett," she said finally.

"Oh yeah? My old friends with the forked tongues. Can't you find anything better than that to ride with?"

"I'm not riding with them!" she said hotly. "I just—"

A hot blush flew into her face as she broke off. Jim watched her narrowly, checked by her sudden embarrassment. His antagonism melted before a driving curiosity.

"Just what the hell are you doin' out here?"

"Watching them," she answered, keeping her voice even and her glance on the ground.

"Do they know you're here?"

"No."

"Trailed 'em, huh? What for?"

Marilyn looked up with a hot resentment, and again her face flamed. She obviously didn't want to answer; but Jim maintained a cool silence, knowing from past experience that it would force her to speak. "I just wanted to find out something," she said at last, looking back at the ground.

"For instance?"

"Well, that nasty crack you made. I didn't believe it and I wanted to find out for myself—whether or not Grant was mavericking other people's calves."

Jim's heart bounded. Then she hadn't wholly believed him a liar! The shameful doubt in her voice rippled over every tender string in his system, and he asked gently, "Did you get your answer?"

"No, I—" As she looked up, her eyes flashed suddenly beyond Jim and widened with instant terror. Then she screamed. "Jim! *Look out!*"

CHAPTER EIGHT

J IM was moving with the first flash of warning in Marilyn's eyes, whirling, stabbing a hand for his gun. He saw Ace and Bennett stepping away from the rocks, steadying their guns in deliberate aim; and, with the momentum of his spin, he threw himself savagely to the side, Marilyn's scream blending with the crash of guns as he went down.

He slammed two shots at Ace as he was falling and saw the man fold over, mortally hit. Then Jim landed hard on his left side, momentarily jarred off balance. A bullet kicked dirt into his face and he rolled flat, swinging his gun on Bennett and firing by instinct. At his third swift shot, the dark-faced cowboy staggered back, tripped over a jutting rock, and fell out of sight behind the granite jumble.

Jim lunged to his feet. One glance at the crumpled Ace was sufficient, and in four long bounds he reached the rock behind which Bennett had fallen and jumped it, his gun ready for another shot. Bennett lay face down, his gun inches from his motionless hand. Jim kicked the gun out of reach, then grabbed the man's shoulder and pulled him over. He was out cold, blood streaming from a wound high in his right shoulder, a gash on his head showing where he'd hit the rocks when he fell.

Gun still in hand, Jim stepped back over the rock and pulled Ace part way over. The man was dead, as he had suspected, and he was not pretty. One of Jim's slugs had taken him in the chest and the other in the face, smearing the bandage that had been taped over his broken nose. Jim laid him back, face down, and straightened slowly, pulling in a breath that hurt his chest.

Only then did he look at Marilyn. She had ducked aside when the shooting started but now stood frozen, her face chalky, her lips parted. Her blue eyes were fastened on him with an incredulous, horrified stare; and Jim felt that look go clear through him.

"I guess you know," he said slowly, "that it'd be me layin' here if you hadn't yelled."

Her only answer was a convulsive shudder. Jim stood irresolute for a moment, wanting to thank her, but he couldn't tell from her expression how she felt about this. Maybe her horror was due to the fact that she'd seen a man die. Maybe, he thought bleakly, it was because her scream had been an involuntary shriek of terror—that she regretted.

Abruptly he turned back to Bennett, automatically reloading his gun before sheathing it. Then he knelt beside the cowboy, pulling his shirt away from the wound and seeing that it was not a serious one. The bullet had come out on top of the man's shoulder, leaving a clean hole that was bleeding freely but not dangerously.

Swiftly but carefully, Jim tore the cowboy's shirt off and ripped it into strips, fashioning a couple of pads, which he placed over the two mouths of the wound. A part of his mind went over the events leading up to this explosive incident, and he realized that Ace or Bennett, perhaps both, had seen him when he rimmed out of that wash and had trailed him here.

He was preparing to bind the pads tightly into place when he became aware, suddenly, that Marilyn was leaning against the rock directly above him. He looked up, startled. Her face was still pale, but the look of horror had gone out of her eyes, giving way to a strange, deep thoughtfulness that Jim found vastly disturbing.

"You'd patch him up," she said queerly, "after he tried to shoot you in the back?"

"What'd you expect me to do?" he retorted. "Take him down to the creek and drown him?"

"But if he gets well, he'll kill you."

"He'll try. Maybe next time I can shoot straighter."

He challenged her with a direct, piercing stare until her glance wavered and dropped. Then he turned back to the bandaging in stony silence.

Marilyn had no more to say; but he could feel her eyes on him, probing into him, and he wondered if she had really believed him capable of fighting a cripple. He couldn't forget for a minute that she had called him a killer. He had just shown her how he went about the business of killing, and he had also made it clear that he would kill again if he had to. Still her silence, suggestive of pregnant thought, gave him reason to hope that her opinion of him was softening.

When he had finished the bandaging, he procured Bennett's gun, unloaded it, and threw it off the knoll, hearing it crash into the brush far below. Then he rolled a cigarette and lit it, inhaling with a deep relish before glancing at her through the smoke. She was still watching him, her lower lip caught between her teeth; and Jim could find no censure in her expression.

"He may sleep for quite a while yet," he said, keeping his voice matter-of-fact. "Let's go look at that herd."

Without a word Marilyn turned away and walked toward a thick patch of brush where she had evidently left her horse. Jim looked after her for a moment before wheeling down the slope to get Cappy, feeling a surge of exultation that he could hardly restrain. He divined that her attitude toward him *had* softened, and the door to her mind was still open.

The herd, containing not over a hundred animals, was starting to scatter. The old cows had found their calves and were now drifting back through the thick oak brush and manzanita toward the mountain. Jim led the way slowly around them, finally pulling up at a spot where they could watch the animals drift past.

He shifted sideways in the saddle, shoving his hat to the back of his head as he draped his reins over the saddle horn and rolled a cigarette. He kept his eyes on the cattle although he was vividly aware of the girl beside him, sitting very straight in her saddle, biting her lower lip as she watched the cattle file past. There was a lot of Ladder stuff in the bunch, mostly yearlings; but there were, also, a good many of Jim's cows with baby calves—JH, Five Drag, even a few wearing the Box S brand.

"They would have cut them out," Marilyn said, her voice sounding slightly strained, "as soon as they got down out of this brush."

Jim made no comment, watching the cattle with hawk-eyed interest until he spotted what he had hardly dared hope to find: a Five Drag cow being trailed by a short yearling wearing the Ladder brand. He took a pull off his cigarette and then gestured almost lazily.

"They didn't do a very thorough job of weanin' on that little bugger," he said dryly.

"That doesn't necessarily mean anything," Marilyn said quickly. "You know, lots of times a yearling will run with a cow that isn't his mother. Just get used to the bunch she runs with—you know."

"Yeah, that's possible," Jim admitted, "but, Marilyn, doesn't it strike you kinda funny that there would be so many Ladder yearlin's here when there aren't many Ladder cows?"

"Yearlings drift around."

"Yeah," Jim said, slightly caustic. "They'll drift back to their home range if they get a chance."

"Not necessarily," she contradicted. "I don't think the Lord Himself can tell what a yearling is going to do."

Jim shifted in the saddle so that he could watch her fully, having seen all that he needed to see as far as the cattle were concerned. "Well, then, does this strike you funny? I haven't got a single yearlin' in this outfit, Marilyn. Not even a JH, and this is the JH home ranch."

"Holmes was losing his stuff, Jim," she said seriously. "There've been a lot of rustlers come into this country since you left. Men like Holmes and Smith and those other fellows, trying to do the work all by themselves in this rough country, just couldn't hang onto their stuff."

"Well, that shore seems to be the truth," Jim said musingly, "but it's kinda funny that a rustler workin' this canyon, for instance, would take the trouble to cut out the Ladder stuff and leave it here."

"I'm not saying they did that," she said hastily. "These yearlings may have just drifted up here since the water got low on the flat. The rustlers didn't dare hit us over on the other side of the valley."

Jim, watching her closely, seeing the deep earnestness in her eyes, had a growing feeling that she was trying to convince herself more than she was him. If she had been arguing merely with him, she'd have lost her temper before this. He looked down at his cigarette, twirling it in his fingers, keeping his face carefully expressionless as he waited for her to continue.

"Don't you see, Jim? Grant has kept a good strong outfit. He's kept our stuff branded, and he's been shipping twice a year. Your dad and Uncle Dave and old Ramón—they couldn't handle the work of Five Drag all by themselves. They couldn't even keep their calves branded, and it's a cinch they couldn't keep their yearlings rounded up. They were wide open for the rustlers to hit."

Still Jim said nothing, watching the play of expression in her eyes. It was the first time she had failed to throw up a guard against him, and he had a heartwarming feeling that she was nearer to him now than she had been at any time since his return.

"This yearling here," she said in a straightforward manner, "may be yours. You know, it's awfully easy to make a mistake in a big roundup. If you think he's yours, let's rope him right now and vent that brand."

Jim grinned broadly. "One yearling," he drawled, "wouldn't make much difference, the shape we're in." He straightened and lifted his reins, feeling good all over. "Maybe we ought to start gettin' Bennett closer to a doctor, huh?"

They found the cowboy sitting up against the rock, haggard and sick, but not too sick to give Jim a venomous glare. Marilyn had nothing to say to him, but she did stay with him while Jim rode down after the two horses.

He had to blindfold Ace's horse before he could lead the animal near the body. Then he untied Ace's slicker from behind the saddle, rolled the body in it, and threw it face down over the saddle, lashing it securely in place.

Bennett started to swear, thickly but viciously, as Jim pulled him to his feet. Jim shook him, hard enough to bring an agonized groan from his lips.

"You keep your filthy mouth shut," he ordered heartlessly. "You got nothin' to cry about."

He boosted the cowboy into the saddle and held him until Bennett got a grip on the fork with his left hand. Then Jim mounted and, leading Ace's horse, led the way down off the knoll and headed as straight as the broken country would permit toward the Ladder ranch.

By the time they reached the flat Bennett was reeling drunkenly, and Jim had to stop and tie him to the saddle. He knotted the reins and draped them over the saddle horn, knowing the horse would follow the others even if Bennett lost consciousness. As he remounted and started on, Marilyn rode up abreast of him. She glanced at him strangely, but she had no comment to make until they had passed the *ciénaga* and were deep into Ladder range.

"Is this safe?" she asked then.

"Nope," Jim said cheerfully.

They were, in fact, dangerously close to the Ladder headquarters. Jim had been riding warily ever since they reached the flat, and his tension mounted with each mile covered, but he could not let Marilyn take that grisly burden home by herself. Besides, he was in no hurry to leave her, feeling as he did that the relationship between them had subtly improved.

"Jim," she said, turning suddenly to face him, "did you rob that stage?"

"No, I didn't," he answered promptly.

"Can you prove it?"

"Nope. I can prove that I came into this country with as much money as I've spent so far, but of course that doesn't prove that I haven't got more stashed away somewhere."

He let it go at that, eying her steadily but not being able to tell whether or not she believed him.

"Skeet Dorman's a friend of yours," she said thoughtfully.

"Yes, he is, but that wouldn't keep him from arrestin' me if he thought I'd done it." He hesitated, then said slowly, "There's something I've been wantin' to ask you, too. Did you by any chance notice that day in town that Rennick was wearin' a gray checkered shirt? A torn gray checkered shirt?"

She flashed a startled glance at him. "Is he the one who took that shot at you?"

"He's the huckleberry."

"Is that why you killed him?"

"I killed him," Jim said evenly, "because he tried to throw a gun on me when I was lookin'."

Marilyn looked down at her saddle horn. Jim noted that her breathing was ragged, but he was not prepared for the undisguised anxiety she showed him when she lifted her head.

"Jim, why don't you stop this business?"

"What business?"

"This—this war!" She made a fierce little gesture that included the whole range.

"You're talkin' to the wrong man, Marilyn. Grant's the gentleman you'll have to take that up with."

"No, he isn't," she said, and there was a plea in her eyes that hit Jim like a sledge hammer. "Grant isn't the one who's doing it. I know he isn't! He's hard-fisted, sure, but he's got to be, Jim. Like with that fence you're building—"

"Got built," he corrected.

She ignored his interruption. "Grant will *have* to fight that fence. Our cattle have got to have water."

"Yeah, and mine have got to have feed," Jim answered, "which they won't get if there's fifty Ladder cows on every spear of grass. That's pure self-defense, Marilyn. I haven't got either the grass or the water to support your outfit."

"But it'll cause trouble," she said earnestly. "It'll cause more killing."

Jim looked away. There was no argument he could offer to that statement because he knew it was true.

"You don't know Grant, Jim," she continued. "He's not hard, really. He's good and clean, just trying to do a good job of running the ranch Dad built up. Maybe you were justified in killing Rennick, just as you were justified in killing Ace. Maybe—" She faltered, then finished with an effort, "Maybe it's even possible that you couldn't help killing Dick, but there can't be any excuse for deliberately running this into further killing now!"

Her words knocked the wind out of him. That she should realize the killing of Dick had been unavoidable was something for which he had prayed during four long years, but for the realization to come now…

"Stop it, Jim, please, before it gets any worse!"

"I can't stop it," he said roughly.

"But you can, if you want to!"

"Wantin' to has nothin' to do with it. Like I told you, Marilyn, I'm just tryin' to save the ranch *my* dad built up. I'm not lookin' for trouble; and there won't be any trouble, at least over the cattle, if Grant'll quit his crowdin'. If you want to stop this killin', stop Grant!"

"Jim," she said desperately, "won't you listen to reason?"

"Not that kind of reason," he replied, fighting to keep his voice level. "It's Grant who's dealin' the cards in this game, Marilyn. I'm just playin' 'em as they fall."

She straightened slowly, her face hardening. "Is that all you've got to say?"

"That's all there is to say."

"You're still trying to blame this on Grant, are you?"

"I'm just tellin' you," he said shortly. "I'm not lookin' for trouble; but I put that fence up to protect my range and I'll fight to keep it up."

Her uncertainty had vanished in the clash of their stubborn wills, and suddenly her temper flared. Her eyes swept over him in a blistering, scornful inspection.

"And you say you're not looking for trouble! You told me that once before, and you had a rifle in your hands when you said it. You went ahead and used that rifle, just as I knew you would, and you'll use it again. Trouble's all you ever have looked for. You're nothing but a cold-blooded—"

"Reckon this is far enough," Jim interrupted coolly, pulling his horse to a stop. "If I get much closer to those trees down there, I'll be nothin' but the ex-owner of a good ranch." He handed her the reins to Ace's horse, then tipped his hat to her with mocking politeness. "Shore did enjoy our little visit," he drawled. "Come over and see me again sometime."

Before she could answer, he reined away, holding Cappy to a walk and riding with an easy grace that gave no hint of the restraint under which he was laboring.

It was sunset when he reached the ranch. He dispatched Ramón with bedrolls and grub for the boys riding the fence, then went into the kitchen with Dave for a belated meal. He was acutely aware of the fact that Dave was watching him with a steady, narrow speculation; but he finished his meal and got a cigarette going before meeting the old cowboy's gaze.

"You and Ramón make a good gather today?"

"Yeah, we did, Jim. We worked that brush pretty thorough and then got those other boys to help us cut back the Ladder stuff at the gate. What the hell happened to you?"

"Nothin' much," Tim said carelessly. "I met Ace and Bennett out at the JH."

"Oh, yeah? What were they doin' out there?"

"Gatherin' cattle."

Dave's eyes gleamed like live coals in the lamplight. "I reckon they know now that you meant it when you told 'em to stay home."

"Bennett's apt to remember it for a few minutes," Jim admitted. "Ace don't care."

"How come Bennett's still got a memory?" Dave demanded. "Were you shootin' downhill?"

Jim grinned. "Uphill, you old goat, and fast."

"Well, we'll get him next trip," Dave said philosophically.

"Yeah. Cattle are balled up around the *ciénaga*. There'll be a good moon tonight, and Grant might try to move 'em. Reckon we'll take turns sleepin' down at the fence."

Dave favored him with a shrewd, penetrating glance. "Where'd you meet Marilyn?"

Jim felt a shock at the blunt question, but he looked up coolly. "What makes you think I met her?"

"Hell! A blind man could see it. Gunplay never chewed you up inside like that."

Jim looked down at his empty plate and said nothing.

"What was she doin' out there? She wasn't ridin' with Ace and Bennett?"

"No."

"Then what was she doin'?"

"Trailin' 'em to see what they were up to."

"Did she find out?"

Jim shook his head. "She saw the herd they were gatherin,'
but it looked all right to her." He hesitated, then said gruffly, "Ace
and Bennett sneaked up behind me while I was talkin' to her. If
she hadn't yelled, they'd have got me cold."

For a moment Dave stared, his eyes wide. Then he planted
his arms carefully on the table and leaned over them, his eyes
glinting with intensity. "That ought to prove it to you."

"Prove what?"

"That she's still in love with you. I've knowed it all the time."

Jim caught his breath and then let it out explosively. "In love
with me, hell! She told me what she thought of me!"

"What she thinks and what she feels are two different
things," Dave said flatly. "She thought she hated you for a while,
after you killed Dick, but she didn't then and she don't now. That
girl hasn't changed one damn bit."

"You're crazy," Jim bit out savagely. "Crazier'n hell!"

"I'm tellin' you, cowboy. Girls like Marilyn don't give their
hearts away more'n once, and she gave hers to you a long time
ago. She got over Dick's death in just a little while, but what really
hurt her was the fact that you never wrote to her. She kept waitin',
and then gradually froze up. I reckon she decided you just didn't
give a damn."

Jim felt as if he were being strangled. He had wondered that
first day if there would have been a chance for him if he'd written. Again this afternoon he had felt, fleetingly, that there was
still something between them; but it was gone again now.

He ran a trembling hand through his hair and said thickly,
"Water under the bridge, Dave. Anyway, she's Eddie's girl now."

"The hell with Eddie!" Dave snapped. "The only reason
Marilyn started goin' with him in the first place was because he
was a friend of yours."

"He's in love with her," Jim said, feeling his self-control
beginning to crack under the agonizing pressure of Dave's words.

"And I guess you ain't!" Dave said hotly. "No, sir! The hell with Eddie. It's you Marilyn's in love with, and you're a damn fool if you don't take her. If you was to ride over there and grab her and kiss her—"

"*Shut up!*"

Jim's chair crashed over as he lunged to his feet, slamming his cigarette to the floor. Dave stood up slowly, his face turning gray under Jim's blazing stare. He lifted a hand hesitantly.

"Jim—God, I didn't mean nothin'."

Jim swung away, ashamed of the passionate fury that still shook him. He swallowed hard, trying to speak and failing.

"Jim," Dave said simply, "I couldn't think any more of either you or Marilyn if you was my own kids."

"I know it, Dave. It's just—Aw, hell! I'm gettin' so I fly off at everybody, but I'm sorry I waited till you got in front of me."

"Forget it," Dave said, with quick loyalty. "You been havin' more than your share of hell lately, and that's all I had in mind, son. Helpin' you out of some of it. You and Marilyn belong together, damnit."

The gruff, kindly voice steadied Jim, and he turned, trying to grin. It was a sorry effort, but at least his voice was once more cool and careless.

"Maybe we belong together, but we've shore got a fat chance of gettin' there. Even if she isn't through with me now—which I still can't quite believe—she'll be plumb through by the time I get through with Grant."

He clamped a hand on Dave's shoulder, and his grin finally came through. "Let's go see," he drawled with wry humor, "if this is the night I make her hate me for keeps."

CHAPTER NINE

THE night, however, remained quiet. Jim crawled out of a bedroll under a mesquite bush at daybreak to find Tommy just riding back from a last scouting trip to the top of the ridge, at the north end of the fence.

"Nothin' doin'," he reported, showing a boyish disappointment. "Grant ain't scared of us, is he?"

Jim laughed. "Don't you believe it. He'll be showin' up before the day's over, unless he broke a leg or somethin'. You go put on the feed bag, Tommy. I'll take a look up there and see what I can figure out."

By midmorning, there was no longer any figuring necessary. From his vantage point on top of the ridge, Jim could plainly see the dust clouds billowing up all over the flat and knew that Grant was gathering a big herd. He had thought perhaps Ladder would bring only the cattle that were already bunched around the *ciénaga,* in an attempt to sneak through the fence. Now it seemed evident that Grant was going to try to bull his way through in a head-on clash.

No, Jim thought with a cold thrill of anticipation, Grant Talbot wasn't afraid of him.

In the afternoon, Dave joined him on the ridge, bringing him a handful of biscuits and a chunk of cold meat. The old cowboy hunkered on his spurs, rolling a cigarette as he squinted out over the flat.

"Bringin' 'em all, ain't he?" he drawled without inflection.

"All he can gather up in a hurry," Jim agreed.

The dust clouds had converged on the *ciénaga* by now, and a thin, dark stream seemed to be pouring from under it, heading toward Five Drag. Ladder was coming.

"He'll have his whole outfit with him," Dave said, as if it were unimportant. "They can go right over the top of us if they want to."

"Yeah, but it'll shore cost 'em somethin', if we're back in the brush with rifles. He might stampede those cattle and knock the fence down, but he might have to hire a new bunch of cowboys to round 'em up with, too."

Dave laughed, the first laugh Jim had heard from him since Long John Dixon was killed. "Damn you, Jim. You're just itchin' to throw down on that outfit, but you be careful. Grant Talbot don't like to pay for what he gets, and don't you forget it!"

The herd came on, creeping across the flat like a stream of ants. Gradually the animals took shape, and Jim could count the riders spaced around them. Fourteen, and he wondered with a tight chill if Marilyn was one of them.

When the point of the herd passed the Lazy L, late in the afternoon, Jim abruptly stood up and turned to his horse. The drive was coming on slowly but steadily, with two men riding point. The bawling of the cattle could be heard, dim but constant in the distance, by the time Jim and Dave reached the wide, shallow canyon where the other four men had gathered.

"He's got one hell of a big herd and fourteen riders," Jim told them bluntly. "You boys scatter out back here in the brush. Get your rifles handy but stay on your horses in case he stampedes that outfit."

"What are you goin' to do?" Dave demanded.

"It'll depend," Jim said, "on what Grant does, but you boys take to the bushes and stay in 'em. Grant'll know you're there, and he might be more careful if he can't see you."

"Jim—"

"Beat it," Jim said, and grinned at the worry in Dave's eyes.

As the men scattered, Jim rode back twenty yards from the fence and reined up behind a towering soapweed that would give him only partial cover. He pulled his rifle from the scabbard but did not lever a shell into the barrel, still waiting to see whether the men or the cattle came first.

The floor of the canyon was broken, a hundred yards below the fence, by a low round knoll that was fairly free from brush. If Grant came on in the steady line he'd been maintaining, he'd round that knoll on the left and hit the fence just below Jim's position. If the riders left the cattle and scattered, trouble might come from any direction.

Jim's eyes grew strained and his breathing grew shallow as he waited, keeping one eye on his horse's ears, knowing that in all probability the animal would spot movement quicker than he would. Then a rider appeared on top of the knoll, and Jim felt the leap of his blood as he recognized Grant Talbot.

Grant hauled up, lifting his arm in a gesture to stop the herd. Almost immediately another rider appeared beside him, and Jim recognized the high, thin shape of a hawk-faced, gun-swift cowboy known as the Parson because of the black garb he always wore. Other riders came in sight, four, five. Then the seven men in a compact body rode slowly off the knoll and approached the fence.

Jim levered a shell into his rifle, taking one last careful survey of the brush on all sides. He was coldly conscious of the seven men who were *not* in sight, any one of whom might be bushed up with a rifle; but the only man he saw, besides the approaching group, was a cowboy who darted through the brush, rope in hand, trying to stop the herd.

Jim turned his narrowed gaze back to Grant and his group, and he waited until the men were in the open just below the fence. Then he reined away from the soapweed and walked his horse toward them, knowing that a hidden rifleman could kill him but taking a cold satisfaction from the knowledge that Grant would have no chance to attend his funeral.

The Parson pulled up at the fence beside Grant, but the other five men stayed behind them, still tightly grouped. Jim stopped five yards from the fence, but the butt of his rifle balanced lightly against his thigh.

"You're trespassin'," he said evenly.

"You got title to this land you've fenced?" Grant demanded.

"Part of it."

"And the rest of it's free range. I got a herd back here that needs water."

"Go dig 'em a well," Jim said.

Grant kept his hand folded over his saddle horn, but he could not keep the glitter of hatred out of his eyes. He was clean shaven, his handsome face as smooth and as cold as granite. Never had Jim felt more strongly the driving enmity that flowed between them.

"I've been usin' Deep Creek for the last two years," Grant stated, his voice rising in challenge.

"Yeah, I see you have," Jim retorted. "There isn't enough feed in this canyon to fatten up a billy goat."

"There's plenty of feed on the ridges. If I don't water out here, I'll have to drive clear on over to Pinal Creek."

"Then you'd better get started."

Slowly Grant settled back in his saddle. "All right, Dixon," he said with icy deliberation. "I'll take 'em over to Pinal Creek, and I'll give you one warning. From here on, keep your cattle off the flat. Since you got this fence built, see that they stay behind it!"

"Shore, I'll keep 'em behind it," Jim drawled coolly, "until it rains!"

For a second Grant turned rigid, his face gray with restraint. Then, with a savage curse, he yanked his horse around and spurred away, his men close behind him. The instant Grant turned, Jim wheeled the roan he was riding and jumped him into a run for cover. No bullets followed him, and he pulled up in the shelter of a cut bank beside Tommy Ryan, who was leaning over his rifle with an air of supreme disgust.

"He was sure nice about that, wasn't he?" the cowboy complained.

"Too damn nice!" Jim snapped. "Keep your eyes peeled."

Fifteen minutes passed, however, in which nothing happened. Jim could tell from the shrill yells of the Ladder cowboys and the shift in the hovering dust that they were turning the herd, pointing it south.

Dave galloped up, still clutching his rifle and looking more grimly worried than ever. "What the hell do you make of that?" he demanded.

"He's up to something, you can bet on that," Jim answered. "Where's Ramón?"

"Shadowin' 'em to see what they're up to."

"Good boy. That's exactly what I wanted him to do."

"So they're goin' to take 'em over to Pinal Creek, huh?" Dave mused. "Gonna crowd Judge Miller a little."

"That," Jim said pointedly, "is the Judge's business. It's shore none of mine. Besides," he added, with memory of the Judge's quick suspicion still rankling, "maybe if he gets his toes tromped on a little, he won't be so damn quick to get cranky with other people. Let's scatter out here a little and see if we can figure out what in the devil Grant's got in mind."

Darkness closed in, however, and they still didn't have it figured out. They prepared a hurried meal at the Bell house, a squat, stone building containing two rooms with a double fireplace in the partition between them. Ramón came back just as the meal was ready, reporting that the Ladder cattle had passed the south end of the drift fence and were still moving in the direction of Pinal Creek.

For a moment no one spoke. Then Eddie expressed the sentiments of all of them.

"I smell a polecat," he drawled, his eyes narrowed in speculation, "but I ain't shore which way the wind's ablowin'."

"It's a cinch Grant ain't givin' up that easy," Dave agreed. "He may double that herd back tonight."

"Yeah," Jim said. "Or he may let the herd go and double the *cowboys* back to tear hell out of this fence. Let's get on the outside of this grub and get back out there."

There was no question of taking turns at the bedrolls. Jim scattered the men, each of them taking something less than a mile of fence and patrolling it constantly. Jim chose the section directly above Lazy L, figuring that Grant might presume the north end of the fence was now unguarded.

The hours crept by with intolerable slowness, and Jim's tension mounted steadily. The very brilliance of the moonlight, throwing a shadow behind every bush, augmented the strain; and the stillness of the night, broken only occasionally by the shrill yipping of a coyote, worked on his nerves until he was stifling even the sound of his own breathing.

He knew with cold certainty that Ladder was going to strike, somewhere.

The roan horse told him where. It was nearing midnight when the animal threw its head up suddenly, its ears pointed with stiff alertness toward the mountain. Jim swung him that way and stopped, seeing the blaze of light but not immediately grasping its significance.

Then it hit him all at once, like a hard fist in the pit of the stomach. They were firing the ranch!

Jim stood up in his stirrups and let out a range yell that would carry at least as far as the Bell place. He waited a few seconds to give the men time to pull up and listen. Then he yelled, "The ranch!"

The roan was not fresh but he was willing, and in four lunging jumps he was into a hard run. Jim rode him with a tight rein, ready at any second to pull him up if he stumbled; but the big horse was sure of himself, maintaining a powerful stride that carried him over the top of any obstacle he couldn't dodge.

As Jim came out on the last ridge that sloped up to the ranch, he saw a rider briefly silhouetted against the flaming hay barn. Then the man disappeared, and Jim was spurring the roan ruthlessly over the last half mile. The barn was gone, flames already shooting through the roof. The whole interior of the bunkhouse was blazing, lighting every window; but only the back end of the main house was afire.

As Jim threw himself off the roan at the front of the house, he saw Eddie coming up the slope with another rider close behind him. With a fierce hope, Jim dashed inside, grabbed a blanket out of the front bedroom, and ran to the kitchen. The back porch, a frame structure that had been tacked onto the adobe building, was blazing furiously; but flames were just starting to eat around the door and windows leading to the kitchen.

Jim tore into them with his blanket, beating them out as they licked at the wooden frames. He heard someone run across the roof, and in a moment a second man crossed it. Real hope surged through Jim then. If they could keep the fire from spreading from the porch roof to the roof of the house, two feet higher, they had it whipped.

It took an hour of stifling, back-breaking work, Dave in the kitchen with Jim while the other four men beat out the flames and sparks that caught on the roof. When it was over, most of the windows in the kitchen had broken from the heat and the roof would undoubtedly leak; but the house was still standing.

It was the only building on the ranch that was. The adobe walls of the bunkhouse reared grotesquely around the smoldering ruins inside them, and even a part of the near corral had burned.

Jim stood in the dimming glow of the bunkhouse, surveying the wreckage and relishing the driving wrath that took possession of him. "Good and clean and decent!" he gritted. "The rotten skunk!"

"You shore named him," Dave said, his voice hard in spite of the weariness that tinged it. "What do you reckon now? Is he puttin' his cattle through the fence?"

"Hell, no! That'd pin this on him, but he may be tearin' it down. As soon as the boys get in with fresh horses, we'll go see. If I catch him on my range tonight, so help me God, I'll kill him!"

Jim's arms and shoulders were burning in half a dozen places where sparks had singed him, but the nagging pain only added fuel to the fire that was burning inside him. With long, savage strides he went after the roan horse and led him to the corral. Dave and Ramón were already unsaddling their tired horses, and Jim was just starting to loosen his latigo when Tommy returned from the horse pasture, sweeping into the corral at a hard gallop and setting his horse up in a sliding halt.

"The horses are gone, Jim!" he blurted.

"Gone?" Jim echoed blankly. His mind was still too busy with the devastation at hand to grasp a new development.

Tommy nodded. "The fence has been cut and the whole damned remuda's gone. Eddie's tryin' to find out which way they went."

Jim's sudden blinding rage wouldn't even permit him to swear. With his jaws locked so hard they ached, he jerked tight the latigo and swung into the saddle, knowing beyond a doubt that this time the horses had been actually stolen. Men unhurried in their getaway would not have taken the trouble to round up a pastureful of horses unless they intended to drive them off. And Cappy was in that bunch.

On the first open ridge beyond the creek, Eddie and Slim had pulled up and were waiting. Eddie lifted one arm and swung it in a significant gesture toward the south.

"Devil's Pass," he said.

Only for a moment did Jim hesitate, flashing a swift glance over his men. Their faces were smudged from the fire and he knew they were tired, but even in the uncertain light of the moon he could see the grim set of their lips and the unyielding glint in their eyes. All they asked was a crack at the men who had done this.

"All right," he said. "Ramón, you keep Tommy and Slim and stay on these tracks, just in case they didn't go to Devil's Pass. Dave and Eddie and I'll cut straight across country and see if we can head 'em off. And don't walk into any ambushes!"

"I follow tracks," Ramón said in his unruffled, reassuring manner. "Slim and Tommy watch the brush."

Jim pulled out with Dave and Eddie right behind him, riding at a stiff trot. It was a long chance, mounted as they were on tired horses; but Jim was gambling that the men who had taken the remuda would not hurry, figuring that the loss would not be discovered until morning.

Dawn was breaking as they slipped around the cluster of adobe buildings and unpainted frame shacks that made up the town of Devil's Pass. The place had started as a respectable stage station, but it was too close to the border to remain respectable for long. The Pinal range here swung to the west, and the stage road wound down out of the mountains on the south, leading to a long, flat valley that formed an easy chute to Mexico, less than fifty miles away.

A mile south of town, Jim cut down out of the brush into the stage road, where one swift glance showed him that the horses had not gone on through. He crossed the road and climbed the rocky shoulder of the mountain, circling around to come in behind a granite outcropping that would keep them hidden from the eyes of the town. There he dismounted stiffly and loosened his cinch before climbing up onto the rock and settling himself in a niche that provided a good view of the town, two hundred yards below.

He was tired, hungry, mad, but he had the patience to wait. And his patience was rewarded.

The sun was not over an hour high when he saw a rider come out of the brush to the north and west of town and jog into the dusty street. Jim felt a cold thrill as he recognized the lanky shape and black shirt of the Parson.

"He came out of Javelina Canyon," Dave murmured. "That's where the horses are, as shore as hell."

"Wouldn't be surprised. Wonder how many men he's got with him. It wasn't the Parson I saw last night. That fella was wearin' a white shirt."

"Don't matter how many," Dave grunted. "Ramón and the boys are gettin' close by now."

"He was trailin' by moonlight," Eddie reminded him dubiously.

"Yeah, but moonlight ain't goin' to slow that Yaqui down much."

Jim watched narrowly as the Parson dismounted before a ramshackle, two-story building that housed a saloon below and sleeping rooms above.

"Old Grant don't miss any bets, does he?" he muttered. "He had the Parson there at the fence with him last night to give him an alibi. He couldn't have burned the ranch, 'cause he was drivin' cattle to Pinal Creek!" As the Parson disappeared inside the building, Jim settled back and rolled a cigarette. "Let's see who all he comes out with," he drawled with grim speculation. "He's got his buyer all lined up, and we might as well make a clean sweep."

In a few minutes the Parson came back, pausing on the edge of the porch to roll a cigarette. At the same time, three men went out the rear of the building, entered the stable, and reappeared shortly with their horses. Then the four men rode leisurely out of town and disappeared into the brush.

Jim lost no time in following, dropping down off the mountain and cutting the trail the Parson had taken into Javelina Canyon. There he pulled up, eying the spur of the mountain that hemmed in this brush-choked canyon. The ridge was broken, a couple of miles down, by a low saddle.

"That's where the horses came in," he mused. "That's where Ramón will come in, and it's where Ladder will go out."

"Yeah," Dave agreed. "I know this canyon, Jim. It don't go anywhere, but there's a good grassy pocket down there a ways, with a spring. They'll hold the horses down there today and bring 'em out through the pass tonight."

"And in the meantime we'll circle around and pick up Ramón and make shore the Parson and his little playmates don't sneak out on us."

When Ramón and the boys arrived at the saddle, Jim scattered them, sending some of them around to cut off retreat up or down the canyon while he and Dave went straight down.

"Go in slow and easy," he ordered, his voice hard. "If we can surprise 'em, I wouldn't mind stretchin' my rope."

He and Dave made their way cautiously to the bottom of the canyon, holding their horses to a slow walk to give the other boys time to get into position. They were almost to the edge of the grassy clearing when a sharp burst of gunfire sounded up the canyon.

With a yell, Jim spurred into a run toward the sound, plunging into the clearing and flashing a swift glance over the Five Drag remuda milling around in it. There was not a man in sight; but as he swept across the clearing, two riders burst out of the trees directly ahead of him, riding low over their horses' necks and shooting as they came.

Jim felt the jar of a bullet slamming into the fork of his saddle as he swerved the roan aside, firing swiftly at the foremost rider. He hit the man but didn't stop him. The next moment the roan gave a convulsive jump, squealing in pain, then bogged his head and started bucking. Jim had a glimpse of the second rider going down under Dave's withering fire, but the first one made it to the trees and disappeared.

Then Jim had to turn his entire attention to the bawling, bucking horse under him. He spurred the animal ruthlessly, shoulder and flank, but he didn't get the roan's head up until he stumbled over a rock hidden in the grass. Jim whirled him toward the lower edge of the clearing. He was just in time to see Ramón come into sight, the man Jim had shot dragging at the end of his rawhide lariat.

Eddie and Slim had reached the clearing from above to report that they had killed the third of the strangers.

"Where's the Parson?" Jim demanded.

Eddie jerked his head toward Devil's Pass. "When we first came into the trail, I saw where two men had gone out not so long ago."

Jim gritted his teeth against the driving desire to spur on up the trail right then. He knew the roan was tired out, although the grazing wound across his rump was not serious.

"Let's make a rope corral, quick!" he said tightly. "I want those skunks!"

With Cappy under his saddle, Jim made short work of the trip out of the canyon. Eddie and Dave managed to stay with him, but the other men, swearing in futile protest, had been left behind with the horses.

At the edge of town Jim pulled up, the tight cramp releasing its grip on his chest as he saw the two saddled horses in front of the saloon. With the object of his vengeance in sight, he grew suddenly cool and contained. Loosening his gun in the holster, he walked Cappy toward the saloon, Dave and Eddie on either side of him.

As he pulled up at the hitch rack, he heard a laugh inside the building and the door swung open. The Parson, looking back over his shoulder, started to step outside. Jim had just a glimpse of the man behind him, a cowboy wearing a white shirt. He saw the flash of fear on the man's face. Then, with instantaneous reaction, the cowboy shoved the Parson outside and slammed the door.

As the Parson staggered, off balance, he caught sight of Jim and froze, his body twisted awkwardly.

"Howdy, horse thief," Jim said coolly.

The Parson's slaty glance dropped to the horse Jim was riding and for a moment hung there while his thin face turned gray. Then he threw himself violently to the left as his hand stabbed for his gun.

He was fast, incredibly fast. Jim, reaching for his own gun, knew instantly that he couldn't match that draw, and he spurred Cappy sharply, jumping him ahead and then jerking him up short as his gun cleared the holster. The Parson fired twice as he and Jim were both moving, but the bullets went wide. Then Jim flicked his gun up in a snap shot that took the Parson through the heart.

The man stopped, arrested in midstride, although his finger on the trigger jerked convulsively to fire the gun a third time. Jim, his thumb on the hammer, held his next shot, seeing that the Parson was finished. With his eyes setting blankly, he stumbled forward three halting steps before the stiffening went out of his knees and he toppled to the ground, face down.

Eddie was already off his horse and running for the door, gun in hand. As Jim vaulted to the ground, a gasp from Dave stopped him, jerking him around. The old cowboy was bent over his saddle horn, tightly clutching his left side, and Jim could see the blood trickling through his fingers.

"Dave!" he cried, and leaped to grab the old man and pull him bodily out of the saddle.

CHAPTER TEN

"JUST—bounced off a rib," Dave panted, as Jim laid him on the ground. "Wait'll I get my breath."

Jim tore his shirt open, then sank back on his spurs, wiping a sleeve across his face, which was suddenly pouring sweat. Dave had been right. The Parson's last wild bullet had glanced off a rib, cutting only a shallow furrow through the flesh. From the way Dave was breathing, Jim figured the rib was cracked; but he knew the old cowboy was not seriously hurt.

"My God!" he breathed hoarsely. "Scare a man to death, why don't you?"

He hurried to get a couple of towels from the bartender and had the wound nearly bandaged by the time Eddie came back, his face dark with anger.

"That other jigger got away," he groaned out. "Got a horse out of the stable and headed south, runnin' to beat hell."

"He won't come back," Jim said shortly.

Eddie gave Dave a careful inspection as he rolled a cigarette. "You ought to learn to duck, Dave," he drawled.

"You go to hell," Dave retorted.

The men got a filling, cheering breakfast in the town's only restaurant but decided against lingering in Devil's Pass even though they were worn out. Jim and Dave headed down out of the pass toward Pinal while the others took the horses back to the ranch.

In town, Jim left Dave at the doctor's office while he hunted up Skeet Dorman, who was sitting in the Mescal reading a month-old newspaper. Jim told him in detail about everything that had happened.

"That's for the record," he finished, "just in case."

"Doggone, Jim," the deputy complained. "You're depopulatin' my bailiwick. You keep on and I'll be out of a job."

"You still got plenty of stuff to work on," Jim retorted. "There's still the little matter of where my cows went."

"Yeah." Skeet glanced sidelong at the bartender, then leaned over the table and lowered his voice. "You didn't find anything that would prove where the Parson got his ideas, did you?"

Jim shook his head. "Grant's still in the clear."

"Well, be patient, Jim," Dorman advised, with a significant glance.

Jim grinned at him. "You haven't got a hoosegow to put me in, anyway," he drawled, as he stood up. "Don't overwork yourself, Skeet."

He sauntered back outside, pausing on the walk to run his glance idly over the wide, dusty street. At this hour of the day it was practically deserted, and the town had a sleepy look, deceptively peaceful. Someday, he thought grimly, that peaceful look would not be a lie. It was a good little town, and, with a few exceptions, it was filled with good folks.

Jim rolled a cigarette, then led his horse across the street and entered Miller's store. The Judge was holding down his customary post behind the tobacco counter; but not until he was clear inside did Jim see Marilyn, who had evidently left her horse out back. She was standing near the dry-goods counter on the left side of the room, with Donna waiting on her. Both girls looked up, startled, as he entered.

Jim hid his own shock behind a quick grin, touching his hat brim with brief courtesy before turning toward the Judge. He heard Marilyn say, "I'll pick that up later," and heard her start for the door.

"What was that big fire out at your place last night?" the Judge asked.

Jim leaned his left elbow idly on the counter, shoved his hat to the back of his head, and drawled coolly, "Ladder burned me out."

Marilyn, reaching for the doorknob, jerked around, staring at him for a moment in incredulity. Then an angry flush spread over her face. "That's a lie!" she snapped.

Jim shrugged. "You know the Parson?"

"Certainly!"

"Wears a Ladder brand, don't he?"

"He's working for the ranch, if that's what you mean."

"*Was* workin' for it," Jim corrected. "He and some brown-headed fella wearin' a white shirt fired the ranch, then stole the horses and sold 'em to three gentlemen up at Devil's Pass."

Marilyn took a short stride toward him, her little fists doubled at her sides. "What makes you think the Parson and Elliott did that?" she demanded.

"Because we trailed 'em," Jim said evenly. "We got the horses and the gentlemen that bought 'em. Incidentally, you better tell Grant the Parson's still up there, in case he wants to bury him."

"What—" Marilyn choked. "What did you do to Elliott?"

Jim merely grinned at her and took a long pull from his cigarette. Marilyn's breast heaved as she dragged in a deep breath and held it, her eyes snapping.

"You bloodthirsty devil!" she burst out finally. "I don't believe a word you've said. Maybe your horses were stolen, but you killed the Parson just because he was working for Ladder!"

Jim turned calmly to the Judge. "How do you like to have Ladder pressin' you?"

The Judge flashed a startled look at Marilyn, then faced Jim angrily. "Now listen here, Jim—"

"You got a plow?" Jim interrupted.

"What do you want with a plow?"

"I want to dig out a long trench for the bodies," Jim said soberly. "I haven't got the time to keep diggin' individual graves."

He glanced casually at Marilyn as he said it and saw that his gibe had gone home. She whirled toward the door, her hair flying; but she stopped short as Dave entered, the splotch of dried blood on his shirt visible.

"Uncle Dave, you're hurt!"

"Shucks, little one, I'm all right," Dave said with a grin. "How you doin'?"

"What happened?" she asked anxiously.

"Got in front of a bullet, is all."

"A bullet!" she echoed. "Who shot you?"

Dave closed the door carefully, then tipped his hat far down over his eyes. "The Parson."

"Was he trying to kill you?" she asked, horrified.

"No, ma'am," Dave said gravely. "He was tryin' to put some holes in Jim, but he was half a second too slow."

"You mean—he drew on Jim?"

"Uh-huh. Just as soon as he saw the horse Jim was ridin'. I reckon," Dave added mildly, "his conscience was bitin' him."

Marilyn flashed a swift look over her shoulder at Jim, then turned back to Dave with a helpless little gesture. "Golly, Uncle Dave, I'm sorry about this. But I'm sure Grant didn't know anything about it."

"The hell he didn't," Dave said bluntly. "Marilyn, I think the world of you and I wouldn't hurt you for anything, but that brother of yours is a first-class skunk!"

Marilyn turned as still as a rock, and Jim felt himself grow tight with a sympathy he dared not show. She would listen to Dave where she would not listen to him, and he hoped fervently that she would believe.

Dave lifted a hand and opened his mouth, as if wanting to undo the damage he had done; but Marilyn shook her head, a short, savage little jerk. Then, without a word, she brushed past him and hurried outside.

"Damn me," Dave grunted, wiping a hand across his lips, "I shore talk a lot, but I reckon I ain't sorry. I never could figure out how she stayed so sweet and pretty when she was stuck in a corral with a bunch of polecats."

Jim, the devil of perversity knocked out of him by Marilyn's reaction, turned abruptly to Miller and became all business. "You got a plow I can borrow? I want to build a dirt tank."

"Why in the hell didn't you say so a while ago?" the Judge snapped irritably. "Yeah, I got one."

"Be all right if I send Ramón down after it tomorrow?"

The Judge nodded. "Send him down."

"Thanks."

Jim, turning to go, became aware suddenly that Donna was staring at him with a queer, uncertain light in her eyes. The expression checked him, flooding him with a hot embarrassment. He remembered, vividly, having seen that same expression on Eddie's face when they were discussing Marilyn; and it was partly to allay Eddie's suspicious jealousy that he sauntered toward Donna now, grinning as he lifted one leg over the edge of the counter and sat down. He was grateful to Dave, who immediately engaged the Judge in conversation.

"Have they set a date for that dance yet?" Jim asked.

"Yes," she said, eying him dubiously. "It's next Saturday."

"A week, huh? I ought to have things in pretty good shape by then, and I'll shore be needin' a vacation. You reckon you'd go to the dance with me if I'd ask you?"

The uncertain light in her eyes vanished before a sparkling eagerness, and her face turned rosy. "Why don't you ask and find out?" she asked tartly.

Jim grinned. "I shore hate to stick my neck out, but I reckon I got nerve enough. Will you go with me?"

"I'd love to, Jim."

She said it simply, with only a faint smile to lighten her earnestness. Jim stood up, taking a moment to look into the depths of her eyes, feeling the warmth of her loyalty and love go through him like a strong drink. His misgivings melted under her direct gaze, and his grin broadened.

"I'll be seein' you," he drawled. Abruptly he swung toward the door, calling out to Dave, "Come on, you old *bandalero*. Let's go home."

Dave fired a number of inquiring glances at him but asked no questions as they rode out of town. The old cowboy was weakening from the pain in his side, and when they reached the Bell place he rode slowly on toward the ranch while Jim turned along the fence. He found where it had been cut last night, but the cowboys had repaired it after they brought the horses back through. Nowhere else had the fence been touched.

"I reckon," he said grimly to Cappy, "that Grant figures he did enough damage last night. Maybe he'll kinda back up and take it slow for a while now. Give us a chance to build that tank."

The thought encouraged him; and, as he rode in to find Eddie, Slim, and. Tommy setting new poles in the corral that had been burned, his confidence soared. One glance at the horse pasture showed him that that fence, too, had been repaired.

"For hell's sake," Jim said, surprised and pleased beyond expression. "Save some of it for tomorrow. Let's take on a load of grub and go to bed."

"Just which bed," Eddie drawled, straightening to eye the ruins of the bunkhouse, "would you prefer?"

"Ramón go after those bedrolls at the Bell place?"

"Yeah. He brought 'em up a while ago."

"Well, come on in the house," Jim said gruffly. "We only got two bedrooms, but we got a lot of nice hard space on the living-room floor."

The next morning Dave admitted that he felt like the tag end of a bad stampede, and Jim prevailed upon him to stay in bed.

The rest of them, however, started to work on the tank. While Ramón went after the plow, Jim and the boys built a drag with which to move the loosened dirt. It was a crude affair, a six-foot section of a big log, split lengthwise, with a chain fastened to the ends, to which they could hitch a team. They rigged a stout handle in the center so that they could keep the flat side of the log moving into the loose dirt.

"If we can get the tank done this week," Jim told them, "next week we'll move up onto the mountain and do some cowboyin'."

With that to encourage them, the men tore into the job of building the tank just as they had torn into every other job that had confronted them. By the following Saturday noon the work was finished, the depression deepened enough and the dam high enough to hold a good lake of water.

Jim dug a shallow spillway around the lower end of the dam so that a chance overflow wouldn't erode the face of it. Then he inspected the layout with satisfaction and said, "If we can get just a little rain at first, we'll run a herd in here and trample that right good. Then we'll really have something."

"We shore will," Eddie agreed with pride. "We get that thing full, it'll water a lot of cattle." He paused, glancing sidelong at Jim before asking, with a slight strain in his voice, "You goin' to the dance tonight?"

"Shore am. Are you?"

"I reckon."

Jim ran a hand over his stubbled face and said casually, "I shore got to clean up, too. Donna might change her mind about goin' with me if she saw me like this."

Eddie flashed him a startled glance. Then he laughed, a quick, joyous sound that told more about his feelings than did his dry words. "Well, you couldn't blame her much for that. You look about as kissable as a cactus patch."

Dave, who had been doing nothing strenuous during the week and now felt pretty good, decided to go with them; but the other three men elected to stay at the ranch. Jim left his horse in town and walked the short distance through the orchard to the Miller house.

Donna was ready and waiting for him, dressed in a white gown that brought an instant grin of appreciation to his lips. He noticed the intent expression in her eyes, but she said nothing until they were outside, walking through the mottled moonlight toward the long frame building where the dance was being held.

"Jim," she said then, nervously, "aren't you carrying a gun?"

"A gun?" he echoed. "To a dance?"

"I was over at the store a while ago," she said hurriedly, "and saw Ladder ride in. The whole outfit. Grant was in the buckboard with Marilyn and he was wearing a dark suit, but I thought I saw a gun under his coat."

Jim grinned at her. "Don't go lookin' under my coat, young lady."

She caught his inference and smiled her relief, but she couldn't immediately free herself from the nervousness. "I hope there won't be any trouble."

"There won't," he assured her. "Skeet'll be there, and maybe Brady and his outfit. Grant won't start anything in town."

Jim himself was nervous, although not at the prospect of trouble with Grant. He couldn't remember a dance in this town at which he had not been with Marilyn. Thought of watching her now in someone else's arms, out of his reach, put a tight, chilling cramp in his chest; but he determined with stubborn pride to make this evening a pleasant one.

As he entered the hall with Donna, he saw Dave and Eddie a short distance away, talking to Dorman. Then, beyond them across the room, he saw Grant, eying him with an insolent stare. Jim ascertained immediately that the man was carrying a gun, all right, but his mind refused to dwell on the fact. Marilyn stood beside her brother, wearing a dress that was no bluer than her eyes, her fair hair gleaming like pure silver in the soft lamplight.

At the sudden pressure of Donna's hand on his arm, Jim glanced down at her.

"Oh, Jim," she said fearfully. "The way he looks at you!"

"Shore, he's a friendly sort of a jigger," Jim returned lightly, "but what's worryin' me is the way these cowboys are lookin' at *you*."

Donna laughed and, as Jim swung her into the first dance, her anxiety gave way to a sparkling gaiety. She was an excellent dancer, and Jim tried to concentrate his attention on her alone; but he found, repeatedly, that his eyes were straying around the room in search of Marilyn.

The presence of Grant evidently kept Eddie from approaching her, but Jim watched jealously as she danced with one after another of the Ladder cowboys. As the evening progressed and he had to release Donna to other clamoring partners, he found himself growing tense and unreasonably angry.

Never once did he catch Marilyn looking at him. She was ignoring him completely, a fact that gradually ate into him until he was as touchy as a disturbed bear.

It was growing late when Jim, having just danced with Mrs. Brady, turned back toward the floor and saw Marilyn approaching, her head high, her glance focused on a point slightly to his left. He stopped short, flashing a look that way and seeing Dave and Eddie not over five feet from him. Marilyn walked straight up to them, smiling warmly.

"How are you, Uncle Dave?"

"Fit as a fiddle," the old cowboy replied with a broad grin. "I haven't done anything all week except a little cookin' for the outfit."

"Well, I'm certainly glad." She flicked a mischievous glance to Eddie, then looked back at Dave. "I was beginning to wonder if you two mavericks weren't going to dance with me."

"Well, God bless me!" Eddie blurted with a happy laugh. "Dave, after me you come first."

Jim turned stonily away, found Donna, and swept her onto the floor. It was a fast dance, which fed his violent mood, and he soon had Donna laughing breathlessly. He saw Grant stalk across the floor, his face gray with anger, and leave the building. Then the dance ended and someone—he didn't see who—took Donna away from him.

Jim stepped to the door and smoked a cigarette, staring fixedly off into the night as he blew the smoke out of him with sharp, explosive breaths. He could not forget the pleasant warmth that had filled him that day at the JH when Marilyn had seemed to be leaning almost imperceptibly toward him. Nor could he forget the queer, uncertain look she had given him in the store after Dave had backed up his story about the fight in Devil's Pass. That she should refuse even to look at him now was more than he could stand.

He did not turn away from the door until the orchestra swung into the next dance, a smooth but fairly fast waltz. As he came around, he saw Dave and Marilyn just a short distance away. Dave had his hand on the girl's elbow, guiding her toward the edge of the floor with apparent aimlessness while he held her attention with some story that had her laughing.

Only for a fraction of a second did Jim hesitate. Then in three long strides he reached them.

"My dance," he said, and swept her onto the floor before she could protest.

He whirled her through the other dancers on the floor, feeling the firm grip of her hand on his shoulder, sensing the lithe grace of her body as she instinctively fell into step with him. He couldn't bring himself to look at her; but the faint perfume of her hair worked its way through him, softening the harsh drive that had made him grab her. Unconsciously his arm tightened around her.

He felt her stiffen. Then deliberately she shoved him back, continuing in step with him but holding herself coldly aloof.

"What did you do to Elliott?" she demanded coldly.

Jim glanced down at her for the first time. "Didn't he ever come back?" he asked innocently.

"You know very well he didn't, but I guess you didn't expect them to find his body, did you?"

"His body?" Jim echoed, startled.

"What was left of it. Grant wouldn't tell me what you had done to him, but he said it was horrible, inhuman. You tortured him to death!"

Jim turned to ice. Maybe someone had butchered Elliott, to pin a murder on him. Or maybe someone had merely lied. He said narrowly, "Just where did they find that carcass?"

"Right where you left it!" she flared, her eyes daring him to deny it. They were still dancing, but Marilyn was as stiff as a ramrod in his arms and Jim was moving with the music only from force of habit. "The bartender saw you tie him up and ride off with him, so Grant started hunting for him."

Jim had his answer, and a blazing wrath welled up in him. Grant, he thought savagely, must have been as sure as he was that the brown-headed cowboy would never come back. "So Grant told you I murdered Elliott, did he? I suppose he told you, too, just what the Parson and Elliott were doin' in Devil's Pass that day."

"Certainly he told me. He'd sent them up there to find out how much water there was in Javelina Canyon, and he had sent them up there just that morning. They hadn't been anywhere near your ranch. The men who stole your horses burned your ranch, and you knew that when you killed our boys!"

Jim pulled in a hissing breath, then snapped his teeth against the blistering answer he'd been about to make. The adamant light in her eyes told him that she wouldn't believe him, anyway. Grant had seen to that, turning her once more flatly against him. Jim's hatred for the man swelled over him like a tidal wave, destroying the last vestige of his self-control.

"And to think," she said, her lip curling, "that I had about decided you killed only when you had to. To think I ever doubted Grant! He told me—"

"Grant again, huh?" Jim abruptly stopped dancing and let go of her, stepping back to sweep a withering glance over her. "Your darlin' brother," he said in deliberate, acid tones, "does an awful lot of talkin' but there's one thing wrong with it. It happens that he's a goddamned liar!"

Her nostrils flared as she caught her breath. Then her lips flattened and she swung her right hand in a swift, stinging slap. For a moment Jim didn't move, watching her with cold defiance, giving her time to hit him again if she wanted to. When he saw she wasn't going to, he made her a slight, mocking bow, then turned and strode stiffly way, leaving her standing alone in a circle of shocked, gaping dancers.

CHAPTER ELEVEN

Jɪᴍ stalked outside, elbowing his way roughly through the knot of cowboys around the door. His face still burned from the slap Marilyn had given him, but that was as nothing compared to the fire that raged inside him. He moved away from the building into the shadow of towering cottonwoods and rolled a cigarette, pacing back and forth restively as he smoked it.

He had just flipped it way when Donna approached him hesitantly. "Jim," she said in a small, faint voice, "would you like to go home?"

"Let's."

He took her arm and led her away from the dance hall into the orchard that lay between town and the Miller house. Donna said nothing, and they had covered half the distance before Jim realized that she was trotting to keep up with him. Abruptly he pulled up and looked down at her, shame-faced.

"Hell," he said.

She laughed in embarrassment. "That's all right. Times when a person needs to move fast."

He took her hand and started on more slowly, struck once more by her quick, unquestioning loyalty. He only said, "Thanks for savvyin'."

She didn't answer, but her little hand tightened its grip on his. Jim didn't look down at her again until they stopped on the wide front porch of the house. Then he faced her reluctantly.

A ray of moonlight touched her face, accentuating the darkness of her eyes; but he could see the thoughtful, almost somber expression in them.

"I'm sorry, Donna."

"Forget it," she said with a faint smile. "I had a wonderful time."

"Yeah, I'll bet you did! But I appreciate your goin' with me, even if I couldn't make myself behave like a gentleman."

"Times," she said, "when a man can't act like a gentleman and still be a man."

Her face was tilted up to him, and he could see that she was waiting, wondering. He pulled her suddenly into his arms, the back of her head cradled in his big left hand. For a moment he stared down at her, knowing she wanted his kiss, knowing, too, that he couldn't give it to her. Swiftly he bent his head and touched his lips to her hair. Then he wheeled and jumped off the porch, heading for town with long, tight strides.

He had hurt her, and he knew it. He hated himself for it, but he would have hated himself more if he had allowed his kiss to lie to her.

Dave and Eddie had already picked up their horses and evidently had gone home. As Jim swung into his saddle, he saw the Ladder buckboard pull away from the dance hall. Without a second glance, he reined his horse away from the hitch rack and spurred him into a hard gallop out of town.

There was no light showing in the house when he reached the ranch, still in a bleak frame of mind. He rode into the corral, unsaddled his horse, and tossed the saddle onto the fence, afterward turning the animal out into the pasture. Then he turned toward the house.

As he stepped through the corral gate, he became aware, suddenly, of a man leaning against the big oak tree just beyond. He stopped short, his hand starting up under his coat.

"It's me," came Eddie's voice.

Slowly the cowboy shoved away from the tree and strode out into the moonlight, his thumbs hooked in his crossed cartridge belts. Jim saw those gun belts, which Eddie had put on after returning to the ranch, and the cowboy had removed his coat.

"What's up?" he asked quickly.

"I'm not shore." Eddie's hat was pulled low on his head, shielding his eyes, but his voice was edged. "What happened between you and Marilyn?"

"Marilyn?" Jim echoed.

"Yeah. What the hell was the idea of grabbin' her for that dance and then walkin' off and leavin' her in the middle of the floor?"

His blunt question burned into Jim like salt in an open wound. Unconsciously he squared off, hands on hips. "Is that some of your business?" he bit out.

"I reckon it is," Eddie replied in even, hard accents. "As far as I know, Marilyn's my girl."

"You didn't take her to that dance!"

"I couldn't take her, but she asked me to be there. Besides, I'll look out for her anywhere, any time, whether she's with me or not. Now I'm askin' you—what the hell was the idea of walkin' off and leavin' her in the middle of the floor?"

Jim tried to get a grip on his rising temper. He didn't want to fight Eddie, but he couldn't keep still. He said harshly, "Did you expect me to keep on dancin' with her after she took a swing at me?"

"That's what I'm drivin' at," Eddie said, his voice carrying a deadly ring. "What did you say that made her slap you?"

"None of your business," Jim snapped, and started past him.

Eddie shot out a hand, clamped it over his shoulder, and spun him around. Jim, what little restraint he felt going up in a blaze of fury, knocked the hand away and caught his balance, ready to swing; but Eddie had stepped back.

"I'm makin' it my business, cowboy," he said tightly. "I'll knock the hell out of any man that insults that girl!"

"I didn't insult her."

"Then why'd she slap you? Marilyn isn't the kind of girl to take a swing at a man unless she is insulted."

"Marilyn," Jim said flatly, "is the kind of girl who'll take a swing at any man she doesn't like, and she doesn't seem to care much about me!"

"Maybe," Eddie said through his teeth, "she's got good reason."

Jim took a long stride forward, his fist doubled. "You're talkin' too much, Eddie, and I won't take it. If you don't like me, say so. I'll pay you off and you can get the hell off this ranch!"

For a moment Eddie stood rigid, the muscles in his jaws corded. Then slowly the tension eased out of him, and he lifted one hand in a vague gesture. "I do like you, Jim," he said, his voice ragged. "That's why I was hopin' you'd tell me you hadn't insulted her. Any other man, I wouldn't have stopped to ask him questions."

His words pulled Jim up short and left him speechless.

"I told you once," Eddie went on more calmly, "that you were the only pard I ever had, and that still goes. If you want to fire me, all right; but I wouldn't quit you in the middle of a fight like this. Hell, I—"

He broke off, shaking his head and looking at the ground. Jim let his breath out in a sigh as the anger washed out of him and left him suddenly bone tired.

He ran a hand wearily over the back of his neck and said. "You're right, Eddie. That was a scurvy trick to play on any girl and I shouldn't have done it, but I didn't insult *her*."

Eddie looked up, watching Jim closely, but he didn't comment. Jim dragged in a deep breath and forced himself to go on.

"She gave me hell for what happened up in Devil's Pass. Grant told her I butchered that fella that was with the Parson just because he was a Ladder cowboy. I—kinda blew up. Told her Grant was a goddamned liar."

"Jiminy," Eddie breathed. "No wonder she popped you."

"Yeah. I asked for it."

"Why'd you dance with her?" Eddie asked curiously. "She'd made it kinda plain that she wasn't interested."

"Too plain," Jim said. "I was wonderin' what was bitin' her." He forced a grin. "You know, when you're fightin' a war, it sometimes helps to know what the enemy's got in mind. I could see that she thought I'd done somethin' a lot worse than I had, and I wondered what Grant was up to. I found out."

"Ye-e-ah. Did somebody kill that cowboy?"

Jim shook his head. "Just some more of Grant's lies." He hesitated, then said slowly, "Eddie, I reckon I owe you an apology, both ways from the jack, but it'll never happen again."

"I hope not," Eddie said gruffly.

"I'm not about to fire you, and if you're not quitting—"

Jim finished by extending his hand. Only for a second did Eddie hesitate. Then he took the outstretched hand, and they turned toward the house, with nothing more to say. Eddie went on into the living room, where his bedroll was spread on the floor, while Jim turned into the back bedroom.

He stripped off his clothes and eased into bed carefully, thinking Dave was asleep; but he had hardly settled himself when the old cowboy rolled over and spoke softly.

"Eddie wait for you?"

"Yeah."

"What'd he want?"

'Nothin' much."

Jim lay flat on his back, staring at the darkened ceiling, but he could feel Dave's eyes on him.

"He was sore," Dave said. "Never said a damn word all the way home."

"Well, you can't blame him."

"The hell I can't," Dave said, getting a good deal of vehemence into his voice even though he kept it soft. "It's none of his business if you and Marilyn want to fight."

"Yeah, I reckon it is," Jim said slowly, pulling a decision out of the misery that was eating into him. "He's in love with her, and I reckon I'll lay off of her."

Dave reared up on one elbow. "Don't be a damn fool!" he snapped.

"Look, Dave. Eddie and I came awful near to fightin'. I invited him to pull out, but he said he wouldn't quit me in the middle of a fight."

"Not if there's somethin' in it for him," Dave said shortly.

"He's willin' to help me," Jim said, still with a dull weariness.

"What you mean is he's willin' to help himself. Eddie Worthington," Dave said, spacing the words deliberately, "is lookin' out strictly for Eddie Worthington, and don't you forget it!"

"You got him wrong, Dave. He's my friend and Marilyn's his girl, and that's the way it is. I'm not goin' to have anything more to do with her."

Dave's breath hissed sharply in the darkness, and Jim expected him to blow up; but after a moment he threw himself violently over onto his side, his back to Jim, and jerked the blanket up around his shoulders. Jim kept right on staring at the ceiling, trying to think but finding that his mind was a blank wall.

By 10 o'clock the next morning the Five Drag outfit was ready to pull out for the mountain. Three pack horses were loaded with bedding, grub, cooking utensils. Dave leaned disconsolately against the corral fence, one boot heel propped up on it, his hat pulled low over his eyes.

Eddie grinned at him and said cheerfully, "That's what you get for layin' off that tank-buildin' job."

"You go to hell," Dave grumbled. "My side's all right."

"Not for the kind of ridin' we'll be doin' on that old moun-tain," Jim contradicted. "My Lord, Dave. I'd think, after all the years you put in battlin' the brush and rocks up there, you'd be glad to stay home."

Dave tilted his head back and squinted up at the mountain, ranging his eyes over the jagged ridges and timbered backbone. He didn't answer, but Jim read that look.

"You be patient," he told him gruffly. "We're just goin' to take a ride up there now, for a week's look-see. If there are enough cattle up there to make it worth while, we'll be goin' back later, after your side is plumb well."

"Yeah, all right," Dave conceded. "Jim, your best bet is to go up to Turkey Spring. There's an old trap around the water there that might not be in too bad shape."

"We'll look her over," Jim nodded, swinging into his saddle. "Take it easy now, you old *bandalero*. We'll see you at the end of the week."

Dave grinned. "I'll be so damn lazy by that time I probably won't even be cookin' for myself."

Jim laughed as he led the way out of the corral and turned up the canyon, the other cowboys, driving the pack horses and extra saddle horses, falling in behind him. He turned at the last bend from which the corral would be visible and lifted a hand to Dave, who was still leaning against the fence, watching them go.

Then he turned his attention to the country around him, feel-ing a certain exhilaration at riding back onto the mountain after four years away from it. It was a rough piece of country that had taken a grim toll of broken legs and necks, but Jim had always liked it, perhaps partly because of that. It presented a challenge, both to man and to horse.

Mesquites and sycamores gave way to oak brush and manza-nita as the floor of the canyon sloped up toward the notch. Then came the pines. Jim climbed into the notch, then swung to the right, gradually rimming up to the top of the mountain, reveling in the crisp, pine-scented air that presented such a contrast to the warm smell of the desert far below.

He rode leisurely, choosing the easiest way for the pack horses, following generally along the top of the mountain but skirting the high, jagged bluffs. He saw deer, bear, turkey; and he saw cattle.

By the time they reached Turkey Spring, late in the afternoon, his exhilaration had grown into a genuine enthusiasm. He had seen literally hundreds of head of cattle that had drifted up here during the bad years on the flat and, because of conditions, had been left unmolested. Most of the old cows carried one or another of the valley brands, including a good many Ladders; but all of the younger animals were mavericks.

While the other men unloaded and hobbled the horses and made camp in a little clearing above the spring, Jim looked over the big pole trap that had been built around it. It was not in bad shape, and one day's work would make it strong enough to hold even the wildest of the old cows.

When Jim returned to camp, Ramón looked up from beside the fire and grinned widely. "I see lotta Five Drags," he said ruefully. "Guess Dave and I not so good cowboys."

"There's a lot of everything," Jim said.

"Well, you're not alyin'," Eddie said in feigned disgust. "If I'd known there was this many cattle up here, I'd have bought a runnin' iron and gone into business for myself."

Jim hunkered on his spurs beside the fire and rolled a cigarette. "There's enough cattle up here," he said with hard emphasis, "to stock all five of those ranches of mine, if I can brand 'em and hang onto 'em—and stay alive."

"Well, we'll do the brandin'," Eddie drawled. "Hangin' onto em' and stayin' alive may be up to you." He paused, squinting at Jim uncertainly. "You gonna be delicate about this?"

"Delicate?"

"Yeah. There's a lot of Ladder cows up here, along with some others that ain't wearin' your brands."

"Well, I'm not goin' to be too delicate," Jim said bluntly. "We won't brand any sucklin' calves unless we know, positively, that they belong to one of our own cows. That kind of evidence has a habit of runnin' around. But we'll shore as hell slap a Five Drag on everything that's weaned."

"Fair enough," Eddie grunted, and all three of the other men voiced their assent.

"Some folks," Jim said dryly, "would call that rustlin'. Maybe it is, but under the circumstances my conscience ain't goin' to keep me awake one little bit."

Turkey Spring was in an ideal location for a cattle trap, lying as it did at the head of a canyon just under a natural depression in the backbone of the mountain. Cattle trying to get away from either direction would pass it, and expert riding and last-minute spooking could shoot them into the trap before they saw it. The trap itself was built back into the timber and was invisible from the wings that led to it on either side of the spring.

Jim and his men cut holes and repaired the fence. Then, on the next day, they saddled up.

Eddie expressed the feelings of all of them.

"By golly, I'm shore ready to start swingin' a rope. I been swingin' pliers, shovels, and axes till I'm near ruined."

Jim started out keeping a tally of the stock he branded, but he soon lost track of the count. He did know, as the days passed, that he was getting the Five Drag burned onto an encouraging number of cattle—weaned yearlings, big steers, two—and three-year-old heifers and cows, some of whom had calves of their own, which were also adopted into the outfit.

The wild, fast work fed Jim's need for violent action—a need that he'd had to hold in restraint. He was thoroughly enjoying himself and was relishing a growing confidence until Saturday morning, when he discovered a strange rider who seemed to be shadowing him. He was in a deep canyon at the time, and he caught just a glimpse of the horse passing into the timber on the ridge high above him.

Jim gave no sign of his discovery, continuing to ride slowly until he was sure he was out of sight behind a dense mass of brush and rocks. Then, staying under cover, he spurred up the canyon for half a mile before rimming out on the ridge, well above the spot where he had seen the rider. He found the tracks of the man's horse and followed them warily, knowing that it could not have been a Five Drag cowboy.

He passed the place where he had seen the man, but still the tracks led on, angling down the ridge toward the flat, far below. Jim pulled up on a rocky point, scanning the country with minute care, and finally saw the man, now down in the canyon and riding away fast.

Jim scowled darkly as he watched the rider out of sight, wondering what it meant. As soon as he got back to camp, shortly after noon, he made a careful circle of the area and found the same horse track within a quarter of a mile of the spring. Deeply thoughtful, he rode back to the trap, where the other men were waiting for the branding irons to heat, and told them about it.

Eddie was the first one who spoke, slowly. "It might be just some jigger headin' for the border, who didn't care to be seen on the way."

"Ladder," Ramón said without expression.

"That's my hunch," Jim admitted. "Grant sent somebody up here to find out what we're doin'."

"Well, what the hell?" Eddie said. "We haven't put a brand on a damn thing he can prove is his."

That was true, but Jim could not shake off the uneasy feeling that had settled over him. "He knows we're all up here on the mountain now, or will know it by evenin'. No tellin' what he'll do."

"He might tear up fence or tank," Ramón said in his soft voice, "just for hell."

"Yeah," Tommy said, his dark eyes wide on Jim. "or plant somethin' on us. He claims Eddie and Slim and I are rustlers, anyway."

Ramón nodded. "Us, too. He even accuse Long John."

Jim, watching them closely for their thoughts, felt a mounting tension. He knew Skeet Dorman wouldn't willingly arrest him; but if Grant planted some kind of evidence and swore out a warrant, the lawman would have no choice.

"We'd shore play hell," Eddie drawled grimly, "tryin' to fight from the inside of a jailhouse."

"Yeah," Tommy agreed with an emphatic nod, "and we might play hell provin' it was a frame-up, too."

With sudden decision, Jim stepped to the ground and jerked tight his two cinches. "Let's brand this outfit and clear out of here. I wasn't goin' out till tomorrow, but one day won't make much difference. If that was a Ladder cowboy, checkin' up on us, it's a pretty good bet Grant's got somethin' on his mind."

They had caught over twenty head of mavericks in the trap, and the work went slowly in spite of the fact that the men were all anxious to finish. Roping in the brushy enclosure was hard, and the big animals had to be heeled and stretched out.

It was late afternoon when Jim shifted his saddle to Cappy and said, "I'll ride on in so I can get a look at the fence and tank before dark. You boys break camp and come on down."

Jim did not take the easier, longer route around by the notch, but turned down the first ridge that tipped steeply down to the floor of the canyon directly behind the ranch. As he passed the corrals, he noticed that Dave had finished the repair work on the one that had partially burned, and he found that the old cowboy had also cleared the debris away from the back of the house.

He dismounted by the kitchen door and stepped inside, calling, "Hey, you!" Then he stopped short, his grin of anticipation freezing as he stared at the disordered room.

One chair was tipped crazily against the wall, a splintered wreck. The table had been overturned, and shattered glass and crockery littered the floor, along with smears of kerosene, sirup, and other foodstuffs. A frying pan on the stove was still smoking, filling the air with the odor of charred meat.

Automatically Jim pulled the frying pan to a corner of the stove as he stepped past, his glance once more sweeping over the wreckage. Then he saw the dark stain of blood splattered over both table and floor, and he lunged toward the living room, yelling.

"Dave!"

The trail of dried blood led to the open front door, but Jim flashed a look into both bedrooms before bounding outside and once more stopping short. The dust of the yard was cut and criss-crossed by the fresh tracks of several horses, and he saw instantly where they had headed out—in the direction of the cottonwood-lined creek.

Gripped by a terrible icy fear, Jim turned and ran back through the house, throwing himself onto Cappy and spurring the horse into a wild run along the trail the men had taken. He was oblivious of the mesquite branches that whipped across his face, riding far over Cappy's shoulder with his eyes on the trail ahead, cursing himself for ever having left Dave alone. He crossed the creek, shot through the willows bordering it on the far side, then pulled to an abrupt, plunging halt.

Not over fifteen feet ahead of him was Dave, his body dangling from the limb of a gnarled old cottonwood, his head twisted grotesquely by the rope that bit into his throat. Pinned to the front of his shirt was a crudely lettered placard: "Rustlers take warning!"

Jim grabbed the fork of his saddle as he stared, refusing for a moment to believe what his eyes saw. Drying blood smeared the front of the old cowboy's shirt, from a new wound high in his chest; but it was horribly obvious that he had been alive and conscious when he was hanged.

"*Dave!*" Jim whispered, with the first stabbing pain of grief.

He closed his eyes and dropped his head, clinging to the saddle horn while he fought off a blinding sickness. Sometime after it passed—he didn't know how long—he dismounted and stumbled to the bush to which the end of the rope had been tied. He eased Dave to the ground gently, as if afraid of hurting him, and as gently removed the rope from around his neck.

The old cowboy had been dead but a short time. His body was still warm and soft with the life that was gone. Jim lifted him in his arms, held him balanced over Cappy's neck while he swung into the saddle, then turned back to the ranch at a slow walk.

As he came out of the brush below the house, he lifted a barren gaze to the grassy bench beyond; and he heard again the voice of his dying dad saying the old bench was due for some new customers. Jim looked down at the still form in his arms, feeling the sharp edge of grief giving way before an icy, deadly resolve.

The bench would get its customer, but it would not be the only cemetery in the country to take on a new burden.

He carried Dave into the bedroom and covered him, pausing for a moment to stare down, tight-lipped, at the expression of agony that had been frozen on Dave's face. With that look searing his brain, Jim turned stonily out of the house and swung back onto Cappy. He glanced once up the canyon without catching sight of any of the other Five Drag men. Then he whirled Cappy and jumped him into a lope.

He paused at the cottonwood only long enough to coil up the rope that had been used and hang it on his saddle before spurring once more into a hard gallop on the plain trail toward town. His killing fury would not even allow him to note how many men there had been in the party.

It didn't matter. The only thing that mattered was that Grant Talbot was going to get his rope back—a split second before he died.

CHAPTER TWELVE

DARKNESS was closing in as Jim pulled Cappy to a walk at the north end of Pinal's main street, lifting his bleak glance from the tracks he had been following to the bunch of saddled horses standing before the Mescal. He loosened the gun in his holster, letting his horse walk on down the street as his left hand closed hard over the rope he had brought with him.

He passed Miller's store, aware that someone stood on the walk before it but neither knowing nor caring who it was. Slowly he rode past the line of tethered horses, his eyes ranging over each saddle in turn. Then he pulled up, his lip curling in a slight snarl as he stared at Grant Talbot's saddle. The rope strap hung loose, empty.

He lifted his glance over the swinging doors to the lighted barroom, feeling the pulse of an insatiable hatred as his eyes found Grant. The man had his hat shoved far back on his blond head and was laughing as he lifted a drink to his lips. The men around him were but blurred images in Jim's vision.

He turned back, putting Cappy in at the rack short of the line of Ladder horses. He stepped to the ground, Grant's rope in his hand, and tossed his reins over the rail. As he laid hold of the rail to vault it, he felt a hand touch his arm and he swung around, his gun in his hand and his thumb on the hammer before he saw that it was Marilyn.

He sheathed his gun with a savage gesture and turned again toward the rail, but she grabbed his arm.

"Jim, what's the matter?" she asked tightly. "What's happened?"

He turned deliberately toward her, his breathing ragged as he glared down into her face. Then he jerked his head toward the saloon and said harshly. "They hung old Dave."

"Hung him!" She grabbed the rail convulsively, her lips parted in a gape of horror. "Who, Jim? Why?"

"The tracks," he said, twisting to point without taking his eyes off her face, "lead right straight to that bunch of horses!"

"To that—Oh, no, Jim," she breathed. "There must be some mistake."

"There's no mistake. Take a look at Grant's saddle. His rope's gone!" He emphasized his words by lifting the rope in his left hand and jabbing it at her. "They left a sign on him—'Rustlers take warning.' Dave was no rustler, and you know it. He was nothin' but a crippled old man, and they murdered him in cold blood!"

"Oh, Jim!" Marilyn appeared about to collapse, clinging to the rail and trembling uncontrollably. "What are you going to do?"

He looked her full in the eyes and said brutally, "I'm goin' to kill your precious brother."

He stepped away from her and turned again to the rail, but she darted in front of him, both hands on his chest.

"Wait, Jim. Please. Listen to me! That rope doesn't prove anything. Grant may have lost his rope or lent it to someone. There's nothing on that one to prove it's his."

"Get out of my way," Jim said in low, hard tones.

"Jim, please!" she begged, twisting her hands into his shirt. "I love him. I was waiting to ride home with him." She broke off, shaking her head fiercely. "He's wild, Jim. I know that, but he's not bad. I can see now that he *has* been mavericking other people's calves, crowding. He's been hard when he didn't have to be, but he hasn't done anything really bad."

Jim lifted a cold hand to her wrist, intending to shove her away from him; but she hung on, speaking with desperate haste.

"Jim, help me stop him before it's too late. He hasn't done anything actually lawless yet, and he hasn't been responsible for what the boys have done. But they're dragging him down. They're all in there now, maybe planning other murders without Grant's knowledge. It's just a question of time until he's involved. Give him a chance, Jim. Help me get him away from those men before it's too late!"

Jim had gone very still. He was still staring at Marilyn; but he was seeing, suddenly, the other men in that saloon. "They're all in there…" Up until now he hadn't thought of the other members of the outfit, hadn't, in the merciless grip of his passion, looked beyond the vision of Grant's death. Now he realized with shocking clarity that if he went into that saloon with a gun, he would die, even though he could undoubtedly take Grant with him when he went down.

"Jim, you've got to believe me," Marilyn was pleading passionately. "It isn't Grant. It's those other men, doing things he can't help. Please don't kill him, Jim!"

With cold purpose, Jim forced his mind to call up the blur of faces that had met his eye when he glanced into the saloon. Skeet Dorman was there. Of that he was sure. And Brady. Yes, and Judge Miller, seated at a table.

Marilyn evidently mistook his silence for an indication that he was yielding. Her voice softened. "Help me save him. Please, Jim."

"Save him!" Jim said thickly.

Abruptly he swung toward his horse, unbuckled his gun belt, and hung it over the saddle horn. He was not ready to die, but his fury would not be denied and he knew that Ladder wouldn't dare gun him down in cold blood in front of Skeet and Brady and Miller.

He vaulted the rail and stepped up onto the walk, then stopped as Marilyn once more whipped in front of him, grabbing his shirt.

"Jim, what are you going to do?"

Unconsciously, Jim flexed his big right hand. "I'm gonna take him apart."

"Jim, don't—"

"Get out of my way, Marilyn."

The relentless quality of his voice made her draw back, staring at him with horrified eyes. He could see the revulsion stamped on her face, but even that could not check him. He swept out a long arm and brushed her out of his way, striding past her to enter the saloon.

He opened the swinging doors with a violence that banged them against the wall, bringing instant silence. Jim paused only long enough to see Grant swing away from the bar and stop short, startled. Then he crossed the room, the hard, even thud of his boots making the only sound. With measured care he laid the rope on the bar, watching Grant and seeing the man's instinctive awareness of peril vying with his hatred.

"There's your rope," Jim rasped out, "you murderer!"

Then he struck, a swift blow to the jaw that cracked loudly in the strained silence. Grant jerked back, caught his balance, and leaped at Jim as Jim drove in to hit him again.

Other men jumped away, swearing and yelling. During the first vicious exchange of blows, Jim heard Dorman's voice roar out over the din, "Hold it, Bennett!"

After that, Jim was aware only of the gray face and hard, weaving body in front of him. Grant had a little edge in weight, perhaps a longer reach; but he did not have the memory of Dave's horribly twisted face driving him on. He didn't have the goading thought of a good ranch ruined, of a father heartlessly murdered. He'd had a brother killed, yes; but he knew, just as did everyone in the valley except, perhaps, Marilyn, that Dick Talbot had asked for the death he met.

Jim fought with a cold precision, landing blow after blow that drove Grant slowly backward across the room. Then he stepped in fast, taking a sickening blow over the heart in order to land a solid right that snapped Grant's head back and sent him down. He crashed into a table, which splintered under him, but he rolled clear and bounded to his feet, meeting Jim's rush with a furious onslaught that staggered them both.

Jim hardly felt the rock-hard fists that slammed into him time after time. His bitter fury excluded everything except the desire to smash Grant's face, to feel flesh and bone turn pulpy under his hands. He lunged in again, driving a left into Grant's stomach that brought his guard down and swinging again at the gray, snarling face. He felt his knuckles grind on bone, and the blood flew.

Grant staggered but kept his feet, throwing himself at Jim and grabbing him with both arms, twisting to throw him. Jim drove his forearm into Grant's windpipe and wrenched free; but as he stepped back, his spur tangled in a chair and he went down hard on his back. He rolled as Grant jumped at him, dodging one of the heavy boots but taking the other one with sharp, grinding pain in his side.

Grant lost his balance and fell, but he went down kicking; and Jim staggered drunkenly into the wall as he climbed to his feet, fighting for breath. He shoved himself away as Grant rushed at him, ducking his head and driving both fists into Grant's body. Grant backed away and Jim closed in, lifting a right to the chin and following it with a smashing left to Grant's nose that knocked him flat.

Jim swayed forward, swiping a sleeve at the blood streaming down over his left eye, clouding his vision. As Grant clawed his way up through the tangle of overturned chairs, Jim plowed into him again, giving him no chance to regain his balance. His arms were getting heavy but he swung them doggedly, sending Grant reeling back and flooring him again with a savage blow to the face.

Jim stumbled into a table and caught at it, dragging in painful breaths as he watched Grant slowly roll over. Then he saw that Grant's right hand was fumbling for his gun; and Jim dove onto him, flattening him as he grabbed hand and arm and twisted with all his strength. Grant choked back a yell as he let go of the half-drawn gun, and Jim yanked it out of the holster.

He shoved himself up, threw the gun away. As Grant staggered groggily to his feet, Jim grabbed him and flung him against the wall, where his head rang solidly. Jim fastened his left hand in the remnants of Grant's bloody shirt and held him up while he drove his right fist three times into the hideous, unrecognizable face. Then he jerked him away from the wall and threw him down on his back, falling on top of him and starting a methodical, merciless battering.

He didn't know how long he had been pounding that bloody mask before him when he felt hands on his arms and shoulders, dragging him off, pulling him to his feet. He heard Skeet's voice, barely audible through the hammering in his head.

"That's enough, Jim. My God, you'll kill him! He's out, boy. Now calm down."

Jim didn't even look at the men who'd pulled him up. He wrenched away from them, staggering blindly as he headed for the door. A haze was swimming before his eyes, and his stomach was suddenly writhing. He got outside and made a grab for a porch post but missed, falling into the dust of the street. Slowly he pushed himself up and made his way to Cappy, leaning against the saddle until his head cleared a little and his breathing came easier. Then, fumbling awkwardly, he strapped his gun belt around his waist and pulled himself into the saddle, holding Cappy to a walk as he reined out of town.

One thought remained with him in spite of his sickness: He had to get out of town before Ladder recovered from the shock.

The night was moonless but star-studded, the air cool and soothing against his burning body. His shirt, he discovered, had been ripped practically off him; and he tore a chunk of it loose to wipe the blood out of his eyes. Gradually his stomach settled down; but the pain in his side was persistent, stabbing him with every breath he took. That rib, he knew, was cracked; and a steadily increasing pain in his left hand made him wonder if that, too, were broken. He kept it folded over the fork of his saddle, bracing himself against the swing of Cappy's walk, finding a grim satisfaction in the stiffness of that hand that told of caked, drying blood. Grant Talbot's blood.

Slowly the grip of passion eased its hold on Jim, and he became aware of utter exhaustion. His body came alive, throbbing from the bruises he had sustained, and his muscles stiffened. Twice he had to stop, lying forward over Cappy's neck until dizziness left him.

Opening the gate at the Bell place was an agonizing job that left him breathless and sweating; and he made no attempt to close it, climbing back onto Cappy and riding on toward the ranch. He wondered if Ramón and the boys had made it back yet, or if old Dave were still alone. It would have taken them a while to break camp and load the horses, and they would have had to take the long, easy way off the mountain.

Jim let Cappy pick his own way, knowing he would stay on the trail that led to the ranch. It wound through thick mesquites for a half mile above the Bell house, then dipped down over a low embankment to enter the trees along the creek.

At the edge of the trees, Cappy stopped suddenly, throwing his head up in alarm. The next instant a finger of orange flame darted at Jim from the deep shadows, and he felt a sharp blow strike his chest. It was followed instantly by terrific shock and a rending, tearing pain. He grabbed blindly for the saddle horn as Cappy whirled and lunged back up the embankment.

Jim somehow kept his saddle but he fell forward, his left arm clamped around Cappy's neck, his right reaching for his gun. Other guns were crashing behind him, a continuous roar of sound; and he felt a searing pain across his shoulder.

It was Ladder and he knew it. They had circled around him, knowing he would have to ride slowly. Cappy flashed over the embankment and into the mesquites, and Jim got a hand on the reins, turning him out of the trail. The sudden shift tore Jim apart and he buried his face in Cappy's flying mane, clinging stubbornly. He closed his eyes against the pain that consumed him, and he closed his mind against the certainty that he couldn't get away from them.

He was going out. He could feel the blood pouring out of his chest and back, hot and slippery, and a dreadful weakness crept through him. A thorny branch tore the gun out of his hand, loosened his hold on Cappy's neck. Then the stiffening went out of his legs. He lost the stirrups, but still he hung on until his arms went dead and he could no longer feel the smooth neck of the horse under his hands. Slowly he slid down Cappy's shoulder and hit the ground headfirst, a fall that flipped him over and left him twisted.

For a time he made no effort to move, too dazed and sick to care. He heard horses thundering past at a distance, heading for the gate, pursuing Cappy. Soon the riders would discover the saddle was empty and come back. Then the cracking of brush penetrated the dull film that had slipped over his mind, and he heard a harsh voice yelling orders somewhere back up the creek.

"Pull up! Pull up! Scatter out and watch close. He won't go far. He's hard hit!"

The voice roused Jim and he turned his head, seeing the rim of brush around him and knowing he was lying in the open where they couldn't miss him. The thought of death had never frightened him and didn't now; but the thought of being killed out of hand, like a crippled dog, stirred him to a faint, angry rebellion.

Painfully he pulled himself over onto his face and tried to lift himself on one elbow and a braced hand. The effort took his breath and blacked out his sight, and he sank back against the ground, letting himself go. It wouldn't do any good to crawl into the brush, anyway. They'd find him. He wondered dully whether they would finish him with a bullet or hang him, as they had Dave. It wasn't far to the cottonwoods.

A dull lethargy settled over him, but one thought flickered through his mind and tormented him. He should have left his gun on when he went into the saloon. He could have killed Grant Talbot—and would have, if he'd known he was going to die, anyway. It hurt to know that Grant would still be riding this country when there was nothing left of Five Drag except a huddle of barren graves on the bench.

A hand touched his arm, cold and clammy, jarring him awake. It was coming. Then another hand was laid on his arm, and he was pulled over onto his back. He felt the same cold hand touch his breast over his heart; and he opened his eyes, wondering. Then he blinked, staring, doubting his bleary sight.

Marilyn knelt beside him, her hat gone, her hair streaming as if she'd been riding fast. There was a wild look in her eyes that Jim had never seen before.

"Oh, Jim," she whispered, with a rush of breath. "They're looking for you!"

Jim merely stared at her, bewildered. After what he had done to Grant, why was she kneeling here, whispering? Why hadn't she yelled out her discovery so they could kill him and get it over with?

"Jim, can you get up if I help you?" she asked tightly. "We've got to get out of here."

"Help me?" Jim's voice was faint, and it came only with a mighty effort. "You'd help me after—"

She made a fierce little gesture. "I don't like murder, and that's what it would be if they found you like this. They're frightfully close and the others will be coming back soon. Where's your gun?"

"Lost it," Jim mumbled, closing his eyes wearily.

"Jim, listen to me," she said urgently, grabbing his shoulder. "I want to help you, but you've got to pull yourself together. We're only about fifty feet from the Bell house. If we can make it that far, I'll hide you and go for help. Can you get up?"

Jim stared up at her again, feeling her words and her presence soak gradually into him with the stimulating effect of a strong drink. Then he grinned.

"Shore," he said, as if he were certain of it.

She got her hands under his shoulders and helped him to sit up, steadying him until the first blind dizziness passed. He struggled to his knees. Then she lifted his left arm over her shoulders and pulled him to his feet. Jim staggered drunkenly, but she held him up, her arm tight around his back, and started through the brush.

She had to guide him, gripping him strongly when he lurched, pulling him back on the course she had set. Jim hadn't know that she had so much strength hidden away in her lithe, slender body, and her effort spurred him to his utmost. His head spun sickeningly. He couldn't get any air into his burning chest, but he gritted his teeth and kept going long after his sight had failed him. Then he stumbled and fell heavily, pulling her down to the ground with him.

For a moment he lay gasping, unable to move. He was aware that Marilyn was tugging at his arm, and her voice came to him faintly.

"Come on, Jim. You can make it." She tugged at his arm again and said sharply, "Don't quit me now!"

Her words stung him to unreasonable anger. He shoved himself up, swearing thickly, determined to show her that he wasn't the quitting kind. He couldn't see her, but he could feel her hands grabbing at him, drawing his arm once more over her shoulders. Then they were moving again.

It was an endless, agonizing nightmare to Jim. He lost track of the ground and didn't know whether his legs were still moving or not. Even the feel of Marilyn's hands slipped away from him, leaving nothing but a soft blackness into which he didn't dare sink....

The feel of a cold, damp weight on his chest brought him back and he looked up, seeing first the starlit square of a window above him. Then he saw Marilyn kneeling at his left. She was tearing the shirt sleeve off his arm, evidently trying to get cloth enough for bandages. For a moment he watched her, trying to make out her features in the faint light but seeing only the white blur of her face.

"Did you drag me in here?" he asked finally, his voice heavy.

He saw the shake of her head. "You made it. Lie quietly now."

Jim tried to grin, but the muscles of his face wouldn't work. "I ain't goin anywhere."

"Don't try to talk," she admonished in a whisper. "Save your strength."

She tied strips of his tattered shirt together and passed them under his body, laying another wet pad over the wound in his back before binding them tightly in place. Apparently she had gone to the creek for water after she had brought him here, and Jim wondered about that.

He said, "This is the second time you've saved my life."

"I haven't saved it yet. You're terribly hurt, Jim. You're bleeding so!"

The strain in her voice added to his wonder, and he tried to see the expression on her face. Her eyes were like dark holes that told him nothing.

"Would you care," he asked wonderingly, "if I died?"

She didn't answer, pulling hard to tighten the bandage even more. The cold pressure brought a relief that made Jim stifle a groan, and it was a moment before he could get his thoughts off his painracked body. She fastened the bandage securely, then dipped another pad in the tin can of water and laid it over his bullet-creased shoulder.

"How did you happen to be out here?" he asked, when he could think again.

"I trailed them. They started for the ranch, but when they cut back, I was afraid of this, so I followed. I heard the shots and saw your horse go by."

Jim's mind was as sluggish as a muddy river; but into it, like a piece of driftwood, slipped the positive statement Dave had made when she saved him before. "Why?" he asked. "Why did you care what happened?"

"I couldn't let them murder you."

She stiffened suddenly, jerking her head to one side and laying her fingers over his lips. Jim heard the thud of a horse's hoofs, but he couldn't concentrate on the sound. He wanted nothing in the world so much as to fold an arm around her shoulders and pull her down and kiss her; but he couldn't locate his arms, couldn't command them. His will was a dead thing. He could only watch her, blinking his eyes now and then to clear his blurring vision.

The horse passed by, going downcountry, and Marilyn bound his shoulder with desperate haste. As she tied off the bandage, she spoke in a forced, shallow voice.

"If they had killed you, Grant would have been blamed for it, just as he's been blamed for other things he didn't do. You know he wasn't with them tonight."

Jim closed his eyes, the moment gone. It was still Grant. He was aware that Marilyn stood up, was moving around the room. He heard the scratch of dragging wood and looked up to find that she had moved a homemade wooden couch into position beside him, hemming him in against the wall and shielding him from the door.

She knelt beside him again for a fleeting moment, her hand on his arm. "I hid my horse down by the creek. You've got to have help, Jim, got to have a doctor." She hesitated, then squeezed his arm reassuringly. "I'll hurry."

"I'll be waitin'," he said faintly, and watched the shadowy outline of her body melt into the deeper shadows away from the window.

For a long time after she had gone, he stared up through the window at the remote, twinkling stars. It seemed weeks since he had held Dave in his arms, carrying him back to the house. Weeks since he had brushed Marilyn out of his way in town. She had been utterly revolted by his determination to fight, but that had not kept her from trying to prevent his murder.

As Skeet Dorman had said, she was awful square. She would have done this much, Jim thought, for any stranger; and the thought left him strangely sick.

His consciousness lapsed at intervals, leaving him in a haze as to the passage of time. His lips were dry, his face hot, when he heard a horse approach the house and stop at the door. He heard the creak of leather, the jingle of a spur. It sounded as if there were only one person, and he felt a nagging disappointment that Marilyn hadn't come back. Of course, there was no reason for her to return. She had patched him up and sent the doctor. That was enough.

A match flared briefly by the door, then was quickly shaken out. Dead silence followed, and Jim's senses came wide awake. He heard the faint creak of a board.

Sweat broke out on his face as he strained to listen. He heard nothing more until a thumbnail scratched across a match head, and the light flared directly above him. By its flickering glow, he saw the dark, strained face of Bennett; and he saw the gun glinting in his hand.

Jim froze as the cowboy flashed a swift glance over him, the beady eyes lingering for a moment on his empty holster. Then Bennett laughed, a harsh, rasping sound that lifted echoes in the vacant room.

"I had a hunch," he said gloatingly. "The rest of 'em are all down below, but I found your horse a while ago with a bloody neck and knew you were still up here somewhere."

The match burned down and Bennett shook it out, swearing at his burned fingers. Jim stared up into the darkness, waiting for the bullet to take him, jerking spasmodically at the screech of wood beside him as Bennett dragged the couch out of the way. Another match flamed, and Jim saw that Bennet had sheathed his gun.

"I got to look at you for just a minute," the Ladder cowboy said with a tight, malicious grin. "I got to think about that slug you put into my shoulder and about them names you called me down in the Mescal. I got to try to visualize how your face is gonna look when I get my hands on your throat, 'cause I won't be able to see it, damnit."

Jim held his gaze deliberately steady on the cowboy's face while he tried to summon strength into exhausted, weakened muscles. He could hear, vividly, Marilyn's thoughtful voice: "If he gets well, he'll kill you."

The match burned down, flickered out. The feel of the sulphur was bitingly strong in Jim's throat as he heard Bennett step over him, then come down on his knees, straddling Jim's chest. Jim could see the dark bulk of the man looming over him, and he could feel Bennett's hands feeling their way slowly, almost tenderly, toward his throat. Then they closed around it, the long, hard fingers tightening slowly, deliberately, into a strangling grip.

CHAPTER THIRTEEN

J IM got his own hands up but there was no strength in them, no power to loosen the grip that was choking him. He writhed futilely, his chest bursting, his brain exploding in a white, flashing agony. He lost the feel of Bennett's hairy wrists under his hands and knew he was going out. Then he heard, dimly, a menacing yell.

Bennett let go of him abruptly, and Jim could drag air back into his lungs. Above the rasping sound of his own tortured breathing, he heard, seemingly far away, the report of a gun, two or three shots rippling out almost in unison. Then a heavy weight struck him, smothing him into oblivion.

When he came around again, a lantern burned fitfully, its wick turned very low. By its light he saw Eddie and Slim moving away with Bennett's limp body, which they threw into a corner. Marilyn was once more kneeling beside him, dipping a cloth into a can of water.

"Kinda looks," Eddie drawled as he returned to squint down at Jim, "like we didn't get here none too soon."

Jim tried to speak but the effort was too great. He closed his eyes.

"Take it easy, pard," Eddie said quickly. "Ramón's comin' with the wagon, and Tommy's gone after the doctor. We'll have you home in no time."

The sap had run completely out of Jim. He lay with his eyes closed while Marilyn moved the cool, damp cloth over his face, touching the cuts and bruises with infinite care.

"What happened to him?" Eddie asked softly.

Marilyn's voice was dull. "He and Grant had a fight."

"Oh, yeah? Jim whip him?"

"Yes."

Eddie paused awkwardly, then said, "We'd just got in. Found old Dave and were wonderin' where to look for Jim when you showed up. You—know what happened?"

"Yes," Marilyn said, and made no further comment.

She rode beside Jim in the bed of the wagon on the way to Five Drag, still in silence. Once he looked up to find her watching him, a strange expression on her face, but it meant nothing to him. He was spent, in a daze that registered nothing except the pain in his body.

He was aware, vaguely, of the hands that lifted him out of the wagon and carried him to a bed, and he heard Eddie tell Marilyn that he would take her home; but he didn't know when the doctor came.

He awoke once to see Donna standing beside his bed, staring down at him with dark, anxious eyes. Tommy, hatless with his sleeves rolled up, was there, too; and Jim remembered hazily that Tommy was always there when he woke up. Another time he saw little Doc Adams, wizened and bewhiskered, bending over him, his eyes gravely thoughtful. Jim wondered about that, in a remote sort of a way; and he wondered, too, when he discovered that his left hand was bandaged, what had happened to it.

Gradually the stream of consciousness returned to him, and he finally awoke to find most of the pain gone, leaving a heavy, listless feeling. The doctor was particularly irritable that day, as he was inclined to be when he was trying to mask pleasure.

"How's he doin', Doc?" Tommy asked quietly.

"He's dead," the doctor snapped. "How could he help being, with all the blood poured out of him and your nursing to boot?

But if he should happen to rise out of the grave and holler for food, give it to him."

"Yes, sir!" Tommy grinned broadly at Jim. "You name it and I'll cook it."

Jim ran a hand thoughtfully over the thick beard on his face, wondering how many days it had been. "You reckon you could shave a man without cuttin' his throat?"

"Well, I can try," Tommy said dubiously, "but it might be safer to fill your stomach first, just in case."

That evening Eddie came in, stopping just inside the door to lean against the wall, a cigarette dangling from his lips. He regarded Jim with a cool, speculative stare. "Tommy says you got it made," he said briefly.

"Yeah." Jim hesitated, then asked with an effort, "Did you get Marilyn home all right that night?"

Eddie's only answer was a nod.

"Did you, by any chance, thank her?" Jim asked dryly. "I never got around to it."

Eddie shrugged. "I don't reckon she needed any thanks," he said coolly.

"Maybe not."

Eddie took a drag off his cigarette and blew the smoke out evenly. "Old Skeet was out once, wantin' to know if we'd found anything that would stand up in court."

"Did you?"

"Hell," Eddie said. "I never had time to look, but there wouldn't have been anything, anyway. They don't leave their callin' cards, unless they leave 'em *in* a man."

"Yeah." Jim sighed. "Did you get Dave taken care of?"

"Shore. We put him right beside your dad."

"How many days has it been, Eddie?"

"Ten or eleven. I'm not shore."

Jim hesitated again, studying the cowboy and sensing a reserve in him that had not been evident since before he went to work for the ranch. He had made no move to approach the bed, had not smiled since entering the room. Jim shifted his injured hand said, "Come on in and sit down."

"Reckon not," Eddie drawled. "I'm goin' to take on a bit of grub and go to bed. I just wondered if there was anythin' special you wanted us to do."

"What have you been doin'?"

"Workin the brush here close to the ranch, brandin' a few calves. We figured we better stick around, since weren't anxious to find *you* decoratin' a cottonwood."

His dry remark put Jim at ease. "I appreciate that, Eddie, and I reckon for now that's good enough."

Eddie nodded, lifted his hand in a lazy gesture, and turned out of the room without another word. Again Jim was struck by the cool restraint in the cowboy's manner, but he attributed it to the tension of the past ten days. The hanging of Dave and the ambushing of Jim had shown clearly what any Five Drag man could expect if he allowed himself to fall into the hands of the Ladder outfit.

The constant, cheerful attendance of Tommy was like a good tonic, and in a week Jim was sitting up. Day after day he watched the cloud masses forming over the mountain, and day after day he watched them drift across the sky to disintegrate on the horizon at sunset. Summer was at hand, and already the grasses of spring had burned dry. It *had* to rain, and soon.

"Someday," Ramón said without inflection, "she let go."

The old Yaqui had thinned, and there was a somber light in his black eyes that hurt Jim every time he saw it. Slim, too, was showing the strain. The cowboy had always been quiet, but now he was almost morose. Only Tommy remained in good spirits; and Jim studied him covertly on more than one occasion, wondering if friendship alone had worked this change in the boy.

Jim was up and around by the time the first rain came, a drenching downpour that was accompanied by lightning and thunder that shook the old adobe house. Jim paced the floor, glancing with frequent anxiety down toward the flat, until Tommy ordered him to bed.

"You ain't doin' that tank no good by wearin' yourself out," the cowboy said flatly. "It may not have rained this hard down on the flat. But if it did and the old tank didn't hold, we'll build the damn thing again. Now, go tie yourself to a bedpost."

Jim was at the corral, however, when Slim, Eddie, and Ramón rode in that evening, their hats streaked from water that had fallen through a dusty atmosphere. Eddie dismounted and eyed Jim coolly, reading the question on Jim's mind.

"Some folks," he drawled, "are too damn lucky to live. The tank was just on the edge of that rain."

"Did it pick up any?" Jim asked eagerly.

"A little. We ran a herd in there and she's now gettin' trampled, just like you wanted."

Jim looked up at Ramón for corroboration of the good news, and the old Yaqui nodded.

"She hold. When the big rain come—" Ramón finished with a shrug.

The big rain came three days later, hitting the ranch headquarters again and moving straight down the canyon toward the tank. Eddie was drenched to the skin when he rode in that evening.

"She's full," he said laconically.

Jim, remembering Eddie's enthusiasm at the time the tank had been built, eyed him searchingly for several moments, disturbed again by the subtle reserve the cowboy had been showing him. Eddie had changed; but, for that matter, so had the others.

"All right," Jim said slowly. "Open the gates tomorrow and turn the cattle out. Ramón, you load up your rifle and keep an eye on things. On the cattle down there and, well, on the whole ranch. Grant'll be movin' back down onto the flat, too, and he may have some new ideas."

"What about the rest of us?" Eddie asked idly.

Jim pulled in a slow breath and let it out in a sigh of disgust. "Hell," he said. "I guess you better hang around here for a while longer."

"I'd think so." Tommy said bluntly. "You'd sure last quick in any kind of a fight, and I'd hate to lose you after all the work I put in on you."

Jim went back to his room and stretched out, swearing to himself. He had to admit that what Tommy had said was true, but the forced inactivity was palling on him unbearably. Physical activity, swift and sometimes violent, had been his only defense against thoughts of Marilyn. Now his defense was down, and the result was a driving restlessness that he could hardly contain.

He remembered, vividly, the wild look that had been in her eyes when she first turned him over and was feeling for his heart to see whether or not he was dead. He remembered, too, that she hadn't answered when he asked whether or not she would care if he died. These things, coupled with the sound of her voice when she'd said he was terribly hurt, seemed more significant to Jim every time he thought of them.

Dave had been sure, bluntly and vehemently sure, that she was still in love with him. Jim hadn't allowed the thought then, figuring that she would despise him the moment he so much as laid a hand on Grant. Yet he knew beyond a doubt that she had seen what he had done to Grant that night before she rode out in a desperate effort to save his life.

Jim abruptly sat up and rolled a cigarette. The thought that she might still care for him turned him wild, putting a tremble in his fingers and a knot in his chest that made breathing a painful effort. He couldn't stand the nagging uncertainty, and he vowed then and there that he would find out, once and for all, at the very first opportunity.

With his decision made, Jim found some ease for his tortured mind and could look on the reviving range land with more of the satisfaction he had expected to feel. It rained in some part of the valley nearly every afternoon, and he could see the brown of the flats gradually giving way to a green carpet.

His broken rib and hand had mended. His wound was healed, at least on the outside, and he could feel the strength welling up in him more powerfully with each passing day.

He was sprawled on his bed one afternoon, reading an old magazine, when Tommy stuck his head in the doorway, his face beaming.

"We got company," he announced.

"Who?" Jim asked, starting up involuntarily.

"Donna and the Judge."

"Oh, yeah?" Slowly Jim swung his legs over the edge of the bed and reached for his boots. He hadn't talked to Donna since the night of the dance, when they had parted on a note of strain. That fact, plus his memory of her standing silently beside his bed, filled him with a strange reluctance to face her. "Tell 'em I'll be right out."

He found them sitting at the kitchen table while Tommy poured them each a cup of coffee. Donna's cheeks were flushed as she looked up at the cowboy; and her eyes, when she turned them to Jim, were sparkling gaily.

"Well," she said tartly. "You don't look very sick."

"He's just lazy," Tommy drawled. "You want a cup of coffee, Jim?"

"Please," Jim said, and stepped forward to meet the Judge's outstretched hand.

"Good to see you back on your feet, Jim," the storekeeper said, showing one of his rare grins.

"Thanks, Judge." Jim flicked a glance at Donna and said, "I been kinda wonderin' why you folks didn't come."

"We were out three times while you were so terribly sick," Donna said quickly, earnestly. "I'd have come back sooner, only old Doc Adams informed me sweetly that you needed rest more than you needed company."

"Yeah, I'll bet he was sweet about it!" Jim laughed as he pulled a chair up to the table and sat down. He added apologetically, "I'd invite you folks into the living room, only it's full of bedrolls and boots. We're kinda batchin' right now."

"You're lucky," Donna said pointedly, "to be able to batch. How are you feeling now, Jim?"

Jim warmed, as he always did, to the light in her eyes. He grinned and drawled with satisfaction, "In about four more days, I'm gonna saddle a bronc and ride the tail plumb off of him."

"It's none of my business," the Judge said dryly, "but I'd like to suggest that you look where you're ridin' from here on."

"Yeah, I'll do that." Jim, suddenly uncomfortable, tilted his chair back against the wall and rolled a cigarette. He wondered if these people knew who had got him out of that jam. He lit his cigarette and asked casually, "What's the news?"

"There's not much," the Judge said. He hesitated, then asked, "Doc tell you about his other patient?"

"Grant?" Jim shook his head. "I never asked, and none of the boys been off the place. Did he get all right?"

"Well, his busted arm's healed up. His face is healed up, too, for that matter, but it sure ain't pretty now."

Jim went very still, trying to hide the savage satisfaction that shot through him but knowing that Donna could see it.

"His nose and one eyebrow are just plain on crooked," the Judge went on deliberately, "and he's got a bad scar on his cheek and another one on his chin. He looks like he'd gone headfirst into a meat grinder." Again the old Judge paused, then said forcefully, "Jim, I can't say I didn't enjoy watchin' that. But don't, for God's sake, ever let him get behind you!"

Jim lowered his glance to his cigarette, the Judge's grim warning detracting not at all from his fierce exultation. Dave, he thought tightly, would have enjoyed watching that, too; and it was just the down payment on an account that was long overdue.

He glanced sidelong at Donna to find that she was staring fixedly at her coffee cup, her cheeks flaming. He frowned as he looked at her squarely, wondering what had confused her so. A swift glance at the Judge netted him no information and he looked on to Tommy, who was leaning against the cupboard across the room. Tommy's dark eyes were fastened on the girl with a deep, wondering look that startled Jim into staring.

Tommy, becoming aware of that scrutiny, straightened abruptly, a dark red wave creeping over his face. "You fellers— folks want some more coffee?" he stammered.

For a moment no one spoke. Then Jim dropped his chair legs back to the floor and said evenly, "Fill 'em up, Tommy."

The cowboy hastened to comply, spilling coffee all over the table and mumbling an incoherent apology. Donna darted a quick glance at Jim out of the corner of her eye and smiled uncertainly.

Jim, watching them, knew now that it was not friendship alone that had wrought the change in Tommy Ryan. He was falling in love with Donna, having met her and undoubtedly talked to her at length during those three times she had come out to see Jim. Moreover, Donna was acutely aware of his feeling.

Whether or not she approved of it Jim couldn't tell. To hide the queer, blank feeling that engulfed him, he asked matter-of-factly, "Any other news?"

"The town," she said, striving to be just as matter-of-fact, "has been very quiet since you and Ladder retired to lick your wounds."

Jim looked at his cigarette and said carefully, "Ladder hasn't been in much since then, huh?"

"Some of the men have. Grant didn't come in until yesterday, and Marilyn hasn't been in at all."

"Oh, no?"

Donna looked at him sharply in spite of the easy tone of his voice. Then she said, "Frankly, I've been wanting to talk to her, to find out what all happened that night; but I haven't seen her since she got Grant gathered up and started home with him."

"Maybe," the Judge said, "she's ashamed to come in. That was sure a raw deal they pulled."

Jim, however, couldn't accept that explanation of Marilyn's absence. No doubt she had spent the first part of the interval nursing Grant, but Grant was well now.

Long after the Judge and Donna had headed back toward town, Jim paced the floor restlessly, trying to quiet a growing fear. He wondered, as he had wondered before, whether Marilyn's part in that night's activities had been discovered. If Grant knew that she was the one who had pulled him out of that sure, deadly trap, he might be holding her prisoner in her own home. Or he might be punishing her in some other way.

Jim couldn't bear the thought that maybe Marilyn was suffering for the help she had given him. Grant Talbot evidently had a high regard for his sister; but his hatred for Jim was beyond restraint, and there was no telling what his reaction would be.

Jim held himself in check for three days, during which Tommy avoided him at every opportunity. Jim sensed the cowboy's embarrassment, but he was too deeply worried to give it much thought. On the evening of the third day, in spite of the fact that his strength had not wholly returned, he donned a clean shirt, strapped on his gun belt, and headed for the corral. He had to find out whether or not Marilyn was all right.

The men were still in the kitchen, smoking, as Jim strode through, but just outside the door Tommy hailed him. Jim turned, watching the young cowboy approach hesitantly, his eyes on the ground. Then, as he had done once before, he pulled in a deep breath and faced Jim squarely.

"Jim, I been thinkin'. I guess Donna's your girl, ain't she?"

Jim shrugged. "I took her to that dance."

"Yeah, and she come out here to see you, not me. I didn't want you to think I was tryin' to cut in or was pullin' anything

behind your back. I just met her and got to talkin' to her and—"
Tommy finished with a helpless gesture.

Again Jim had that queer, blank feeling. Donna's loyalty had
been like a ray of sunshine on a cloudy day; but he had offered
her nothing, and he still couldn't be sure how she felt about this.
He rolled a cigarette and said slowly, "A man can't help how he
feels, Tommy."

"Well, that's sure the truth, and apparently I can't help
showin' it, but I wanted you to know I wasn't tryin' to do you
dirt."

"Yeah." Jim lit his cigarette, feeling the irresistible pull of
Tommy's honesty and boyish simplicity. He didn't want to speak,
but he had to. "A woman's heart is hers to give, Tommy. No man
can take it, and—" He grinned. "God Himself can't tell who she's
goin' to give it to."

Tommy's answering grin dwindled away as his dark eyes
searched Jim's face, their expression holding a gratitude that bor-
dered on worship. "Jim, by God—"

He broke off with a helpless sigh and a quick shake of his
head, and Jim clapped a friendly hand on his shoulder before
turning once more toward the corral. He was jerking up the
cinch on Cappy when Eddie sauntered up, his cigarette, as usual,
dangling from his lips.

"Goin' to town?"

"Doubt if I get that far," Jim replied easily. "I'm just restless.
Been laid up too long, I reckon."

"Well, you want to watch where you're goin' or you're apt to
be laid up again."

Jim laughed as he swung into the saddle. "If I'm not back by
Christmas," he drawled, "you can commence to think I'm not
comin'." He lifted his hand and reined out of the corral. Eddie
leaned against the fence, watching him go.

Night had closed in by the time he reached the Lazy L, and
he headed out across the flat at a mile-eating jog trot. A crescent

moon, riding high in the sky, provided a faint, uncertain light. Jim didn't know whether or not Grant kept the ranch guarded, but he doubted it. Ladder's enemies were not strong enough to dare an attack.

His nerves were humming as he approached the dense growth of cottonwoods surrounding the ranch, but he rode bodily into the trees. In their reassuring shadow he pulled up, sitting stock still as he scanned the layout. The bunkhouse, a hundred yards ahead of him, was strongly lit up, and he could hear an occasional voice lifted in a laugh or a curse. The barns and corrals off to the right of the bunkhouse were dark and shadowy.

Jim reined to the left, holding Cappy to a slow walk as he circled the bunkhouse and approached the main house. Marilyn's room, he remembered, was in the front of the rambling old adobe building. He was still deep in the trees when he again pulled up, his heart hammering as he saw the light in her window. He rode half the distance toward it, then dismounted and left Cappy standing in a growth of shrubbery.

It was dangerous, leaving the horse that close to the house. If he were discovered, there would be hell to pay. But if Jim met someone besides Marilyn, he would need that horse and need him quickly. Maybe, he thought bleakly, he would need him even if he met Marilyn.

He left his spurs on the saddle horn and touched the butt of his gun once, for reassurance, before leaving the shrubs and strolling nonchalantly toward the house. He gained the deep shadow surrounding it and put his back to the wall, scrutinizing the yard with minute care but seeing no one. Then, swiftly, he strode to Marilyn's window.

He paused only long enough for one quick glance into the room, which gave him no sight of the girl, then laid careful hands on the window. It lifted with only a slight protest, and Jim pulled himself quickly into the room, flashing a glance around it that showed it was, indeed, empty. He closed the window behind him and pulled the shade, then turned slowly, suddenly aware that he was bathed in a cold sweat.

A lamp burned on the dressing table, its wick turned low. Jim noticed the bright curtains hanging at the window, the gay patchwork quilt covering the bed. It was a pleasant, cheerful room, and its contrast to the barrenness of a bachelor outfit made his heart ache.

A slow step sounded in the hallway, muffled by a carpet, and Jim leaped across the room. He was behind the door, gun in hand, when it opened and Marilyn stepped into the room. As she turned to close the door, she saw Jim and jumped back convulsively, her eyes popping wide, her lips opening to scream.

CHAPTER FOURTEEN

Jᴵᴹ took a quick step forward, pulling in a hissing breath as he lifted a hand to check her. Marilyn's scream froze on her lips, unuttered. For a moment she stood rigid, still paralyzed by the shock even though she had recognized him. Then, slowly, she closed the door and leaned back against it, trembling.

Jim sheathed his gun and wiped a sleeve across his face, heaving a sigh of relief. "Golly, woman," he breathed.

"What—what are you doing here?" she asked, her voice weak from the start he had given her.

"I came to talk a little."

Marilyn didn't answer immediately, brushing a wisp of hair out of her face as she stared at him, struggling to control her breathing. Jim gave her time to recover her composure, letting his eyes roam down over the soft blue dress she was wearing, then touch her hair before returning to her face. He saw, then, that the instinctive fright in her eyes had vanished before a cold hostility.

"I've nothing to talk to you about," she said evenly.

"Yeah, I reckon you have," he said slowly. "Several things."

She shook her head emphatically. "Get out of here, Jim. I've nothing to talk to you about, and I don't want to have anything to do with you."

"If you mean that," he said, stung, "all you got to do is finish that scream you started, and I shore won't be botherin' you much longer." He waited, seeing that she wasn't going to do it. Then he said deliberately, "I had two questions in mind when I came here. I reckon I got the answer to the first one already, but I'll still ask the other. How come you haven't been to town since that night?"

"Grant told me it wasn't safe for me to ride in."

"Safe?" he echoed. "It's been safe enough all these years."

"Yes," she said, allowing her glance to slide over him in measured distaste, "but you haven't been here all these years."

Jim turned as cold as ice. He pulled in a tight breath and drawled sarcastically, "So Grant's been workin' on you again, has he? Does he know what you did that night?"

"Yes, he does," she said, her chin coming up defiantly. "He said he didn't blame me for trying to prevent a cold-blooded murder, but he said it was too bad somebody couldn't shoot straighter!"

Jim straightened his shoulders and lifted his hands to his hips. "I reckon there's no point in thankin' you for what you did when I can see you're sorry you did it."

"If that's the way you feel about it, maybe I am sorry," she said hotly. "I was trying to prove something to you, but you're too bullheaded to believe the truth when it's shown to you. I told you Grant would have nothing to do with murder, and he had nothing to do with the hanging of Dave. He had lent his rope to Bennett that day."

"The hell he had," Jim drawled in mock surprise. "He's shore careful to give the credit to somebody that can't argue about it, isn't he?"

She cut him off with a fierce little gesture. "And he fired every man who had a hand in that ambush!"

"Fired 'em?"

"Yes, fired 'em!" she snapped, her blazing eyes daring him to doubt it.

"Well, I'll be doggoned," Jim murmured, eying her with faint derision. "You got a whole new crew here?"

"Certainly not. Those weren't all Ladder men who were after you. There were only three of our men in the bunch, and Grant fired them just as soon as he found out who they were."

"Oh, yeah? Wanted to replace 'em with men that wouldn't muff the job next time, huh?"

She took a quick step toward him, her fists clenched at her sides. "I don't see how you could have the nerve to face me after what you did to Grant. I told you then he had nothing to do with that murder, but you wouldn't listen."

"No," Jim said, his voice suddenly hard, "and I'm not listenin' now. I've heard all I can stand to hear about that lyin', sneakin' skunk."

She lifted a hand to slap him, but he grabbed her wrists and jerked her close, tightening his grip until she ceased her struggles with a gasp of pain. Then he looked straight down into her face, seeing the shock and the fury and the uncertainty blended in her eyes.

"You used to have a heart and some brains," he told her in hard, even tones, "but all you've got now is a pair of ears to listen to Grant's lies and a blind quirk to believe 'em. Like about that man Elliott. I didn't kill him. He ran, left the country; but you were willin' to believe I butchered him in cold blood just because Grant said so. Now you're goin' to listen to me for a minute!"

"Let—let go of me," she whispered fearfully.

But he only tightened his grip, pulling her up closer.

"Grant Talbot," he said deliberately, "is the rottenest, filthiest snake that ever hit this range, and everybody on the range knows it except you. You said yourself that all this trouble started three years ago—when your dad died and Grant took over the outfit! Strange coincidence, wasn't it? He's a hog, Marilyn, a damned stingy hog that wanted the whole range without payin' for it. So he stole it, chunk by chunk, from men like Holmes and Smith and Bell who weren't strong enough to fight back. He ruined them, drove 'em out of the country. Five Drag was strong enough to fight back, so he started killin'. Some of the cowboys first. Then my dad! Then Dave!"

She opened her lips to protest, but he gave her no chance.

"He hated my guts even before I killed Dick, and that turned him poison mean. It's me he's been hittin' at, and that by itself ought to show you what kind of man he is. Hangin' Dave because he hated me! Breakin' men with little kids because he couldn't get his hands on me! Dad told me just before he died that Grant had to be stopped for the good of the whole country. You asked me, yourself, to stop him, but you didn't know what you were talkin' about. There's only one way to stop a man like him—with hot lead!"

She shook her head savagely. "You're just—"

"I'm just tellin' you," he said coldly. "Your wonderful brother is a worthless, stinkin', yellow-bellied coyote! He wants my hide and he doesn't give a damn how he gets it." He paused, looking deep into the blue fire of her eyes and seeing nothing except the loathing Grant had put there. It drove him to bitterness. "Dave said he wondered how you could stay so sweet and pretty when you were stuck in a corralful of polecats. I'm glad he can't see you now. You used to be loyal and square, but Grant's warped you till you're no better than he is. You're not even true to yourself any more, and you've shore been hateful to me. Grant may get me before we're through, but by God—"

He let go of her wrists and had his arms around her before she could move. He pulled her up hard against him and bent his head swiftly to kiss her with all the harsh, driving passion that was in him. The touch of her lips fired him, and he hardly felt her fists knotted against his chest. He kissed her cheek, her hair, her neck, and then again her mouth, holding her for that one long moment tight in his arms, as he had dreamed of doing.

Then, abruptly, he lifted his head and shoved her away from him, feeling the blood pound hard against his temples, seeing the stricken expression on Marilyn's face.

"Now then," he said harshly, "go ahead and scream!"

Marilyn sagged back against the door, fixing him with a wide stare that verged on horror. Slowly she lifted a trembling hand to her cheek where he had kissed her, her breasts lifting with a long, uneven breath. "Get out of here," she whispered. "Get out of here and don't ever come near me again!"

For a moment Jim stood rooted, eying her stonily. Then he turned and strode to the window, lifting the shade and jerking the window up with a rending screech that could have been heard all over the house. Without even glancing outside, he threw his legs over the sill and jumped to the ground, stalking openly and disdainfully toward his horse.

No one challenged him as he mounted and lifted Cappy into a lope away from the Ladder ranch. It was late when he got back to Five Drag, and he was surprised to see a light still burning in the kitchen. He turned Cappy into the pasture and walked slowly toward the house, entering with reluctance.

Eddie sat at the kitchen table, reading a magazine; but at Jim's entry, he tipped his chair back against the wall and reached for tobacco, eying Jim with narrowed speculation. He was bare-headed, his lean face quiet and expressionless in the light of the lamp.

"How come?" Jim asked, without much interest.

Eddie shrugged. "I was kinda restless, myself. Where all you been?"

Jim jerked his head down toward the flat. "I rode down there a ways."

Eddie lit his cigarette and asked idly, "See anybody?"

Jim tossed his hat at a peg on the wall and sat down, running a hand through his black hair and staring at the floor. The wild fury he had felt had washed out of him, leaving him morbidly agitated. He didn't want particularly to talk, but he didn't want to go to bed, either.

"You look lower than a snake's belly," Eddie said.

Jim forced a halfhearted grin. "Tired, I guess."

"Well, I'm glad you're back. Frankly, I was waitin' up to be shore you got home all right."

"You were?" Jim looked up in surprise, and he was not proof against the open friendliness in Eddie's voice. The cowboy's cool reserve seemed to have melted away. "What made you think I might not get back all right?"

"I trailed you down there a little ways," Eddie admitted with a rueful grin. "I didn't think it was a very good idea for you to be runnin' around alone. But when I saw where you were headed, I decided I better mind my own damn business."

Jim looked at that grin and felt the strong pull of Eddie's friendship. "Thanks, Eddie," he said gruffly.

"Forget it," Eddie grunted. "That was a hell of a long ride for a feller in your condition." He paused, then asked casually, "Did you see Marilyn?"

"Yeah."

"I figured that's what you went down for." Eddie grinned again. "I'm kinda surprised that you're still wearin' your hide after what you did to Grant. Don't reckon she knew how bad he was hurt that night she was lopin' around savin' your neck."

"Guess not."

"Where'd you meet her, Jim?"

"I slipped into her room."

"You went into that house?" Eddie said incredulously. "Jiminy, Jim, what were you tryin' to do? Commit suicide?"

"I had to talk to her. Donna said she hadn't been to town since that night, and I was afraid Grant had found out what she'd done for me."

"Whooee," Eddie breathed in a tone of wonder. "You must think a lot of that girl to walk into that wolf den just to talk to her."

Jim dropped his head. "Can't help it," he said thickly.

"Still in love with her, huh?"

"Yeah."

"Well," Eddie said without rancor, "nobody can blame you for that. She's that kind of girl."

Eddie's friendliness was like a soothing salve, but it could not ease the painful memory of that kiss and Marilyn's reaction to it.

"Hell!" Jim bit out, flipping his hand in a sudden savage gesture. "The only reason she didn't scream was 'cause she didn't want a bloody mess in her bedroom!"

"Scream?" Eddie echoed. "How come? Did you scare her?"

"No, I—"

Jim broke off, running his hand once more through his hair.

Eddie smoked in silence for a moment, then said evenly, "It's too damn bad a girl like her has to be tied up to that stinkin' Grant."

"She loves the damn thing," Jim said bitterly. "I told her what he was like, but she wouldn't believe me. God, I hate to hurt her again!"

"Yeah," Eddie said softly. "Too bad you'll have to."

"I may not. I been thinkin about it all the way home."

"Thinkin' about what, Jim?"

"Grant." Jim looked up, lifting his hand in a helpless gesture. "I can't just deliberately hunt him down and kill him, knowin' the way she feels about him. Unless he forces my hand, I may let him go."

"Oh, yeah?"

"We'll move back onto the mountain and spend the summer brandin' mavericks. Maybe if we get the ranches built up a little, get a bigger crew so Grant can see we're not goin' to fold up, maybe he'll back off and behave himself. If he will, I reckon I'll bury the hatchet." Jim paused, thinking of Dave and his dad. But they were gone. He couldn't help them by killing Grant Talbot. "Marilyn's been through too much already," he said slowly. "If it'll help her for me to lay off of Grant, I reckon I'll do it."

"He might simmer down and act like a gentleman," Eddie agreed, "but I'll have to see it to believe it. When'll we start this maverick business?"

"In the mornin' you and the boys can move up and make camp. I'll hunt up old Ramón and tell him we're goin', then come on up the next day."

"Leave him here to look after things, huh? That's a good idea, Jim. That old Yaqui's too damn slick to get caught, but he'd shore catch anybody else that tried to start anything."

"He still camped down at the Bell place?"

"I'm not shore where he's camped now," Eddie admitted. "He's been movin' around a lot."

"Well, I'll find him and get things squared away tomorrow."

"Yeah." Eddie stood up to stretch luxuriously. "If we're going back up on that mountain in the mornin', I reckon I better get some sleep." He dropped a hand on Jim's shoulder and grinned faintly. "Cheer up, Jim. Nothin's ever as bad as it looks."

Without waiting for an answer, he turned away and strode into the living room, where his bedroll was spread. After a moment Jim blew out the lamp and went into his bedroom, but it was a long time before he went to sleep. Then he slept fitfully and was up at dawn. He had breakfast nearly ready when Eddie came in from the direction of the corrals.

"Where you been?" Jim asked in surprise.

"Wranglin'. I got a horse to shoe before we pull out."

"Hell," Jim grunted. "I thought you were still in there poundin' your ear with Slim and Tommy. Get 'em up, will you?"

It was nearly noon when the boys had their outfit gathered up and were ready to start for the mountain. Tommy swung onto his horse and grinned down at Jim.

"Don't forget," he said pointedly, "that I got a lot of time invested in that carcass of yours. You take care of it."

"I'll try," Jim said dryly.

Eddie rode over to say good-by. "If you're not up there by tomorrow evenin', we'll come back to find out why not."

"I'll be there," Jim assured him. "If I see any of that Ladder outfit today, I'm gonna run like hell."

As soon as the boys headed up the canyon, Jim roped the roan, Rusty, saddled him, and turned the other horses out into the pasture before reining down toward the Bell place. He rode slowly, feeling the drag of fatigue and the heavy, dulling aftereffects of his emotional upheaval of the evening before.

He found Ramón's camp and followed the fresh tracks of his horse along the fence line and up to the point of the ridge from which, seemingly months before, he had watched the approach of the Ladder herd. Ramón rose out of a jumble of rocks, lifting a hand but voicing no greeting. Jim swung off the roan and sat down in the meager shade of a scraggly mesquite, rolling a cigarette while Ramón hunkered on his spurs in silence beside him.

"How's everything goin'?" Jim asked, when his cigarette was lit.

Ramón shrugged. "Lotta cattle down on the flat. No cowboys."

"They're just lettin' 'em run, huh? Anybody been snoopin' around?"

"No tracks. I been ridin'—" Ramón swept his arm in an inclusive gesture that covered the whole ranch. "See nobody."

"They may be workin' over on the other side of the valley," Jim mused. "Our stuff doin' all right?"

"Gettin' fat. Lotta baby calves."

"Well have to slap a brand on them, come early fall. Right now we're goin' back up on the mountain, Ramón. The boys pulled out this mornin', and I'll be goin' up tomorrow. I'd like to have you stick around here and keep your eyes peeled."

Ramón lifted his head to look at the mountain, a long moody gaze that caused Jim to lay a hand on his arm.

"The old ranch'll make it, Ramón."

"Sure," Ramón said softly, then shook his head. "Not the same. Long John—Dave—"

Jim abruptly stood up. "Listen, Ramón. If Grant gets me, you pull out. And don't stop to say good-by to anybody!"

Ramón looked up slowly, a hard, intent glitter in his eyes that sent a shiver through Jim. It was his only answer, but it was plain enough. Jim mounted somewhat hurriedly, lifted his hand in farewell, and turned down toward the flat.

"Damn me," he said to Rusty, suddenly hunching his shoulders. "If that old Yaqui ever looked like that when he was thinkin' about *me*, I'd leave the country."

Jim cut around the end of the fence and headed toward town, still riding slowly but keeping his eyes ranging over the country before him. He knew he was taking a chance of running into Ladder, but his restless urge to see Donna would not be denied. He needed the warmth and the cheer she always instilled in him; and he wondered if, given the chance, she could not make him forget his hopeless longing for Marilyn.

Jim realized poignantly that he had never opened his heart to Donna. Always he had held thought of Marilyn between them, but now he determined to put the fairhaired sister of Grant Talbot out of his mind. She had made it terribly plain last night that continued thought of her could only torment him.

As he rode into town, he glanced sharply at the few saddled horses lining the street and was relieved to find that none of them was wearing the Ladder brand. He put Rusty in at the rack in front of Miller's store and had just stepped to the ground when Skeet Dorman came out of the store, ambled to the edge of the walk, and spat into the dust.

"They told me you kicked the bucket," he drawled in feigned disgust. "I mighta knowed it was too good to be true."

"I'm glad to see you, too, Skeet," Jim retorted. "What do you know for shore?"

"Not a damn thing. Did you get plumb over that little accident you had?"

"Accident, hell!" Jim grinned as he stepped up onto the walk. "Yeah, I got over it."

Dorman tipped his head back to squint at Jim, a quizzical light in his eyes. "They say the law is s'posed to be impartial, and I reckon it is; but I'd shore like to shake the hand that made hash outa Grant's mug."

Jim laughed as he extended his hand, then said, "The boys said you were out."

"Yeah. I went over that country with a magnifyin' glass, but couldn't find a damn thing. Same thing up around the Pass. I been doin' a lot of ridin', trying to find out where these cows are goin', but—" He finished with a weary shake of his head, then looked at Jim again with that quizzical glint. "What kind of violent ideas you got now?"

"None," Jim admitted. "We're goin' to work the mountain and mind our own business for a while. The boys went up this mornin'."

Skeet nodded in quick approval. "Give things a chance to settle down a little. If we take it slow, and I keep alookin' and you keep alivin', we'll whip this outfit yet."

At that moment a voice sounded behind them, low and vibrant. " 'Lo, Jim."

"Hey!" Jim spun on his heel, grinning as he saw the perky expression on Donna's face. "You're the fella I came in to see."

"Oh, hell," Skeet drawled wearily. "There went my girl." Donna laughed at him and he grinned as he added, "I reckon this is where an old coot like me better take himself over to the saloon and buy himself a drink."

He touched his hat to Donna and sauntered off across the street. Jim turned to the girl, noting how the slanting rays of the sun picked up reddish lights in her hair.

"You travelin' or goin' somewhere?"

"I was starting for home."

"Would you let a feller walk a ways with you?"

"Might," she said, "if a feller wanted to."

They turned along the walk, passed the hotel, then cut into a passageway between buildings and strolled toward the orchard. Once away from the buildings, Jim took her hand, relishing its warm, reassuring pressure.

"You look tired," Donna said solicitously.

"Am, kinda." He grinned down at her. "I haven't done any work for so long, I'm plumb lazy."

"You'd better stay lazy, too, for a couple more weeks."

"Oh, no. I got work to do, young lady." He paused, then said casually, looking off through the trees, "That Tommy's a pretty good nurse, don't you know it?"

"He thinks the world of you," she said warmly. "He was telling me how you gave him a job even though he wasn't well thought of."

Jim looked down at her, grinning faintly. "I'm not the only one he likes."

His remark brought a blush to her cheeks, but she looked at him squarely. "He seems like a nice kid," she said, and at the same time gave his hand a slight squeeze.

It was answer enough. They were deep into the trees now, and Jim stopped, taking her other hand and searching her eyes for her hidden thoughts.

"We're goin' to be gone for a while," he said slowly. "That's why I rode in, to see you before I left."

"Trouble?" she asked with quick anxiety.

"No. We're just goin' up on the mountain. Lot of cattle up there."

"You'll be careful, won't you? That's a rough old country to ride."

"I'll shore be careful," he said. "I don't need any broken legs, especially if there's a chance of another dance comin' up."

Her eyes twinkled as a rosy spot appeared in each cheek. "There's bound to be one sooner or later."

"Yeah."

He looked at her lips, fresh and red and smiling. The smile faded as she saw his look and she stood breathlessly still, watching him with wide eyes.

"There's somethin'," he said, "that I didn't do—"

He lifted his hands to her shoulders and she slipped quickly into his embrace, her hands creeping up around his neck. Jim felt their tender pressure as he pulled her close and bent his head to kiss her.

He could feel the warm pulse of life through her body. He could sense the love and promise in her clinging lips, but he just could not respond. Afterward he held her for a moment, his cheek resting against the top of her head while a feeling of utter desolation swept over him.

When he released her and stepped back, he saw instantly that Donna knew. It was there in her eyes, a deep, black pain. His face turned hot.

"Thanks," he said, with an effort. "I'll be seein' you, Donna."

Her answering voice was small and faint. "Good-by, Jim."

Darkness had fallen by the time Jim got back to the ranch. He unsaddled automatically and automatically built the fire to prepare meat, bread, and coffee. His dreary thoughts had no effect on his appetite—and the food had no effect on the depression that had settled over him.

Long after he had finished eating, he sat at the table, smoking one cigarette after another, staring fixedly at the wall. He had hurt Donna twice. He would not hurt her again by seeking her company. It was still Marilyn, and they both knew it.

At a sound from the direction of the living room, Jim looked up, startled, to see Eddie standing in the doorway, a gun in his hand. For a moment Jim stared at him incredulously, then slowly he pushed his chair back and stood up.

"What the hell?" he asked blankly.

Slim's voice spoke behind him, low and menacing. "Don't move, Jim."

Jim stiffened, his right hand well away from his side, his eyes still riveted to Eddie in a dumfounded stare. Slowly Eddie moved into the room, his gun leveled at Jim's belt buckle. Jim heard a step behind him, felt the hard muzzle of a gun ram into his back as his own gun was jerked out of the holster.

"What the hell?" he repeated, his voice turning harsh.

Eddie came to a halt before him, eying him with a cold, deadly stare. "You forgot somethin', Jim," he drawled in hard, deliberate tones. "Forgot that I was in love with Marilyn!"

CHAPTER FIFTEEN

Jim stood rock still, feeling an icy dread steal through him. He was aware that Eddie had a thumb on the hammer of his gun. He was acutely aware of the presence of Slim, behind him; but it was Eddie's eyes that held him. Their familiar reckless sparkle had vanished before an implacable purpose.

"We were doin' all right," Eddie said, in that same deadly drawl, "as long as you remembered that Marilyn was my girl now. You should have kept on rememberin' it."

"What makes you think I forgot it?" Jim asked evenly.

"That little trip you took last night."

"I told you why I went over there."

"Yeah, you told me a lot of things, and I figured out a lot more. You should have stuck to Donna, cowboy."

Jim pulled in a slow breath, studying Eddie's eyes and seeing that the cowboy would kill him without the slightest hesitation. "If you felt this way about it, why didn't you say somethin' last night?"

"I had some plans to make," Eddie drawled. "Just killin' you wouldn't serve my purpose."

Jim felt again that icy dread crawling along his nerves, but he held his voice level. "If you're holdin' it against me for the way I feel about Marilyn, that's between you and me, Eddie. Slim's got no part in it. How come he's sidin' you in this?"

"Slim's my boy," Eddie said, his eyes taking on a glint of hard amusement. "So's Tommy. You did me a real favor when you hired them."

"What do you mean by that?" Jim demanded.

"We three been workin' together for quite a while, and we had a pretty good business goin' till we stopped to become honest cowpunchers."

"Yeah? What kind of business?"

"Any kind that paid off. Like robbin' that stage, for instance, the first night you were home."

"The stage?" Jim echoed blankly. "Did you do that?"

"Shore." Eddie sheathed his gun and rolled a cigarette without ever taking his eyes off Jim's face. "Kinda shocks you, does it?"

Jim felt a slow anger building up in him, overriding his apprehension. "What the hell was the idea of leavin' a plain trail here? Were you tryin' to frame me for that job?"

"Hell no." Eddie lit his cigarette and grinned, a flat, mirthless grin. "I was tryin' to frame Mr. Talbot. I saw him and two of his men leave town and figured they were comin' out here to put a bullet in you. I also figured that everybody in the country would take it for granted it was Ladder that done the shootin'. So Slim and Tommy and I picked up the cash and let Ladder take the credit for it. You never believed they did it, but Skeet couldn't prove they didn't."

"Who ran off the horses?"

"We did, to kill our tracks out of here."

Jim balled his fists as the anger gripped him hard. "You do the shootin', too?"

"No, we didn't," Eddie said flatly. "We were at the corral when that shootin' come off, just like we'd planned to be. Grant was the gent behind that rifle."

"Did you see him?"

"Saw him plain. I didn't know until the next day that it was your dad that got it instead of you."

Eddie's cold, impersonal voice told plainly that he hadn't cared whether Jim got it or not. The knowledge stung Jim and awakened him to a keener sense of peril. Eddie's testimony would hang Grant Talbot, but Jim knew with chilling certainty that Eddie would never give it.

"Let's go," Slim suggested, his voice flat and toneless.

"We got plenty of time," Eddie drawled, his malevolent gaze still on Jim. "Friend Jim's fair bustin' with questions, and I'm goin' to enjoy givin' him the answers. I could even tell him where a lot of his branded stuff went, if he was interested in knowin'."

"You been rustlin', too, huh?" Jim said, his voice rough with suppressed anger. "If you had such a good business goin', why'd you quit it to work for me?"

"Because you were out to get Grant Talbot. I told you I hated him, and I told you why. I shore wanted to help bust him wide open, but I didn't want to kill him on account of Marilyn. That was a little job I was perfectly willing for you to take off my hands."

"You had it all figured out, didn't you?" Jim said acidly. "You were goin' to let me get Grant out of your way while you stood back waitin' for a chance to move in. What changed your plans? The fact that I said I might let him go?"

"That just cinched it. I'd been wonderin', and that told me all I needed to know. What cooked your goose, cowboy, was the fact that you're still in love with Marilyn, and the fact that she's still about half in love with you."

"The hell she is!"

"The hell she isn't. I could see it that night I took her home after you'd been shot. She was arguin' with herself, but the fact that she had to argue proved to me she wasn't plumb through with you. I let that ride and kept stringin' along until last night, when you admitted you were still in love with her. That's where I changed trains, pardner."

Eddie's flat, even words carried the ring of truth; and for a moment Jim forgot the menace confronting him, his nerves tingling to the knowledge that Marilyn did still care for him.

"Now," Eddie drawled, his eyes narrowing, "comes the part I'm really gonna enjoy tellin' you. After you put your poor, heartbroken self to bed last night, I rode over to Ladder and had a conference with Grant."

"With Grant?" Jim echoed, jarred.

"Yeah. That kinda gives you the cold chills, don't it? You know how he hates you, but maybe you didn't know he's about half scared of you. I've known for a long time he was; and I figured that combination of hate and fear would make him susceptible to a nice, safe proposition, even from me. I was right." Eddie paused, watching Jim narrowly for the effect of his words. "I offered to sell you to him, friend Jim, and he took me up on it."

Jim's breathing grew ragged with a fury he could barely restrain. "How much did I bring?" he bit out.

"Ten thousand bucks," Eddie drawled, then added, with a cold, taunting smile, "and a clear trail to Marilyn." He paused again, his smile broadening as Jim's face grew tight. "Grant wants you awful bad, friend Jim. Bad enough to step aside and let me take his beautiful sister, if she'll have me. And I reckon she will, with you out of the way once and for all."

"Not if she ever hears about this," Jim said tightly. "She'll wonder how Grant got me, and it'll leak out someday."

Eddie shook his head, still smiling. "She won't even know Grant got you, but she'll be hopin' that somebody gets you. You're a stage robber, friend Jim, and a coldblooded murderer to boot. You're gonna skip the country, that's all."

Jim flipped his hand in a negative gesture, then froze as Slim's gun rammed again into his back.

"You hold them hands still," Slim said evenly, "or I'll terminate this long-winded powwow."

Jim eased his hand back to his side, but he could not ease the harsh fury that colored his voice. "She doesn't believe I pulled that robbery."

"Not now," Eddie said, "but she will believe it when she finds out you pulled another one tonight."

"Tonight?"

"Yeah."

Eddie was obviously enjoying himself. Jim had known the cowboy was capable of being hard, but he hadn't known there was a streak of stark cruelty in him. The glimpse he was getting of it now turned him cold.

"You see," Eddie drawled, "the boys and I laid low up on the mountain all day. Then this evenin' I borrowed Cappy and robbed the stage by myself, killed the driver and guard, and left a plain trail back here to the ranch. Kinda turns your stomach, don't it? Just to make shore nobody misses the point, we'll drop a few gold coins around here while we're shiftin' the loot into saddlebags, and we'll see to it that Cappy leaves a plain trail into the mountain." He lifted his hands in an expressive, challenging gesture. "She's foolproof, friend Jim."

Jim had turned rigid as he listened. It *was* foolproof. He himself had told Skeet Dorman that Eddie and Slim and Tommy were up on the mountain, working cattle. Their alibi was established, and Eddie had covered his own trail beautifully. When this robbery was discovered, Jim Dixon would be branded a stage robber and murderer who had fled the country, and Eddie Worthington would be in the clear.

As if in echo to his thought, Eddie drawled tauntingly, "I'm just a poor innocent cowboy who happened to be workin' for the wrong man."

"You two-faced skunk!" Jim bit out savagely. "I told Marilyn last night that Grant was the filthiest, rottenest snake that ever hit this range, but I can see now I was wrong."

"Grant'd like to be tough," Eddie drawled, unruffled, "but he ain't got the guts for it."

"Where's Tommy?" Jim's voice was thick with helpless wrath.

"Waitin' up in the canyon with the other horses. You thought you had him weaned, didn't you? But I got a good hold on that boy and I'm not about to let go. He's in this just as deep as the rest of us, and he did just as good a job of pullin' the wool over your eyes. In fact, it was me that told him to get you to hire Slim."

Jim swore a string of vicious curses that brought a grin of pleasure to Eddie's face.

"Better save some of 'em, Jimmy boy," he advised. "You'll need 'em before we get to Hell's Canyon in the mornin'. That's where we're meetin' Grant to deliver your valuable carcass. Then we'll whip ourselves back up to camp, and we'll shore be distressed when somebody rides up to tell us our boss went plumb to the bad and ran out on us."

"Let's quit the palaver," Slim broke in bluntly. "We got a long ride ahead of us."

"All right. You got a hoggin' string?"

"Yeah, I got one."

"Use it on him." Eddie dropped a hand to his gun. "Put your hands behind you, Jim."

Jim made no move to comply. He stood motionless, eying Eddie with a hard, steady gaze until he heard the scrape of Slim's gun against leather. Then he leaped at Eddie, grabbing his arms and aiming a knee at his groin. Eddie twisted his body with cat-like quickness and took the blow on his thigh, but he couldn't wrench his arms free of Jim's grip. Jim ducked his head and rammed it savagely into Eddie's face, staggering him, then swung his body powerfully to throw Eddie between him and Slim.

He didn't make it. Just as he started to turn, Slim grabbed him from behind, getting an arm around his throat and breaking the grip he had on Eddie. He grabbed Slim's arm with both hands and bent forward with a violent twist, throwing the cowboy over his shoulder and sending him crashing into the cupboard. As Jim straightened, whirling, he caught a glimpse of Eddie lunging at him, his gun slashing down at Jim's head. Jim tried to dodge it, tried to get an arm up to fend the blow; but the steel barrel caught him just over the ear and slammed him to the floor.

He tried to get up. He got his arms under him and was trying to lift his spinning, hammering head when a weight drove into his back and flattened him out. The next instant his arms were jerked from beneath him, and he felt the hard bite of a rope around his wrists.

He quit struggling, closing his eyes against the pain in his head and trying to ease his labored breathing. The rope tightened, and a few swift jerks told of the knots being tied. Utter despair washed over Jim. They had him cold, and the thought that they had had to get him through treachery brought but scant comfort.

He heard Eddie's voice, tight and grim. "I figured he'd argue but I didn't know he was that quick, damn him."

"Yeah, damn him!" Slim said painfully. "Why in hell didn't you plug him?"

"And cheat him out of all the nice pleasant thoughts he's goin' to have between now and morning?" Eddie laughed. "You don't savvy how I love this guy, Slim."

The knees that had held Jim down were lifted off his back, and his breathing came easier. He heard one of the men leave the kitchen, but he didn't open his eyes until he was jerked over on his back, his arms wrenched beneath him.

"Now then, damn you," Eddie said pleasantly. "You just lie there and rest while we scatter the evidence."

Slim came back almost immediately, carrying saddlebags and a couple of gray, clinking sacks, obviously heavy. As they poured the gold into the bags, Eddie allowed three coins to drop and roll at random. Then he carried the gray sacks to the stove, poked around in the firebox for a moment, and turned back, grinning.

"That fire's about out," he said with satisfaction. "It'll singe 'em a little, but it won't burn 'em up. Jim, you're shore careless when you get in a hurry. Let's go."

As Eddie pulled Jim to his feet, Slim blew out the lamp and shouldered the saddlebags. Cappy stood just outside the back door, reins dragging. They boosted Jim into the saddle and Eddie swung up behind him, reaching around him to handle the reins. Slim headed up the canyon at a brisk walk, keeping to hard ground that would leave no tracks.

Eddie, however, reined Cappy into softer ground, holding him to a walk as he turned up toward the mountain. For a mile he left a plain trail in the floor of the canyon. Then he turned into the creek and kept the horse in the water as he doubled back toward the ranch, covering half a mile before leaving the creek on hard rocky ground where tracking would be extremely difficut.

"How's it lookin', Jim?" he asked tauntingly. "Think old Dorman can pick up this trail?"

Jim didn't bother to answer. Eddie turned into a thick clump of trees where Slim and Tommy were waiting with the other horses and slid to the ground, handing Cappy's reins to Tommy.

"You lead his bronc. I'll break trail and Slim can ride behind him."

"Yeah. All right." Tommy took the reins, but he hesitated a moment, staring up at Jim with a queer, intent expression on his face.

Jim's lip curled in derision as he drawled, "And Donna said this afternoon that you seemed like a nice fella."

For a second the young cowboy stared, his eyes wide. Then he ducked his head and turned hurriedly toward his horse. Eddie swung into his saddle and turned for a final word to Jim.

"We won't tie you on 'cause this is going to be one hell of a rough trail; but if you try to quit that horse, we'll put a rope on your feet and drag you over this damn mountain."

With that grim threat, he reined out of the trees and turned up the rocky, brushy hillside. Tommy did not look back as he fell in behind him, pulling Cappy along after him.

Jim, staring dismally at Tommy's back, smothered a curse. And he had thought the young cowboy had the makings of a good man!

Eddie followed no trail, taking a circuitous route and deliberately keeping to the roughest country as he worked his way toward the top of the mountain. The cheerless moon provided enough light so the horses could keep their feet, although Cappy, his head pulled up, stumbled time and again.

The air grew cool as they climbed. It felt good on Jim's burning face and damp hair, but it soon chilled his body, aggravating the steady ache that had settled in his arms and shoulders.

Jim knew he was not a coward, but thought of facing Grant Talbot with his hands tied behind him put an icy knot in his stomach and brought out a cold sweat on his face. His death would not be an easy one or a quick one. Grant would exact cruel payment for every scar on his face before allowing his enemy to die.

To keep from thinking of it, Jim turned his mind to Marilyn, grinding his teeth at the thought that Eddie Worthington would get her. If she had turned to him during Jim's absence before, she would surely turn to him now, knowing that Jim would never come back. He wished desperately that there could be some way for her to find out he was dead, but he could see no chance of it. They would kill Cappy, certainly, and they would do a thorough job of erasing all signs of a murder. Jim Dixon and his horse would simply vanish—in the jagged, almost impenetrable confines of Hell's Canyon.

At least he had kissed her; and the feel of her lips was still with him, easing the sharp misery that rode him. Even the memory of her reaction lost its bitter taste in the light of what Eddie had told him.

Jim could see now that Marilyn's loyalty—stubborn, blind, unreasonable, but the more admirable for that—had been divided between him and her brother all the time. She'd been laboring under a terrible strain, fighting herself and fighting Jim because she couldn't believe in both him and Grant. But she had *wanted* to believe in him. That's why she had thrown up to him every lie Grant had told her—because those lies had hurt her. They couldn't have if she didn't care.

Jim, realizing this at last, felt a sharp pang of regret over the accusations he had hurled at her. She was still loyal and square; but, under the influence of Grant's poisonous personality, she was caught in a whirlpool of delusion from which she couldn't escape. And there could never be any escape for her now, sold out to a rotten cow thief by the very brother she loved!

In spite of the dread and desolation he felt, Jim's thoughts gradually converged on Grant. His hatred for the man, made the more savage because of its frustration, was like a snake writhing in his vitals. He could see now that his decision to let Grant go could never have survived the pressure put on him. Right from the beginning, this had had to end with the death of one of them.

The night dragged interminably. Jim's arms grew numb, but he still felt a dull pain in his head and his shoulders ached maddeningly. They crossed the mountain well to the south of the notch and, in a gray, cheerless dawn, dropped down into the tangled country that made up the eastern side of the pinals. Hell's Canyon itself could not be entered from above, and Eddie angled toward it over a jumble of steep ridges and brushy canyons.

In a timbered, grassy hollow just short of the canyon, he pulled up and rode slowly back past Tommy, who reined aside out of his way. Eddie stopped, confronting Jim, and in the light of early day his brown eyes looked rock hard.

"How you doin'?" he asked.

"Fine," Jim drawled, fixing him with a stony gaze.

Eddie's lips twisted into a tight, mirthless grin. "I can see by the color of your face that you been havin' a good time. You're gray, friend Jim."

"I'm tired, friend Eddie," Jim retorted coolly.

"Yeah. Well, I got the remedy for that." His grin faded as his eyes slid down over Jim's chest, touching the left pocket of his shirt before lighting again to his face. Jim felt the shock of that look, and he knew what it meant even before Eddie spoke. "There's one thing I'll do for you, Jim. I'll kill you myself, and do it quick. If Grant got his hands on you, he'd take the hide off you in half-inch strips."

His right hand folded over his gun, lifting it out of the holster with tantalizing slowness. Slim jumped his horse out from behind Jim, jerking his hand up in protest.

"Eddie, wait!" he blurted. "Grant'll raise hell!"

"Let him raise hell," Eddie said callously. "I didn't tell him he'd get a live man he could work on. Friend Jim's goin' to make the rest of this trip on his belly."

He brought the gun up slowly, lining the muzzle on Jim's chest while Jim turned to ice. He could see the flicker of satanic pleasure in Eddie's eyes and knew this wasn't any act of mercy. Eddie grinned again, a taunting smirk, as he folded his thumb over the hammer.

"You want I should give your love to Marilyn?" he inquired in a mocking drawl.

CHAPTER SIXTEEN

JIM felt the heat of blood in his face at the gibe, but he kept his gaze level on Eddie's eyes and said coldly, "You go to hell."

The gun tilted slightly out of line as Eddie eared back the hammer, and he brought it back slowly, deliberately. Jim held his breath, trying to brace himself for the shock when he knew it was useless.

Then, with jarring suddenness, Tommy jerked up a warning hand. "What's that?" he demanded in a sharp, hushed voice.

Eddie flashed a quick glance at him, and Jim reacted to the opportunity without stopping to think. He rammed the spurs savagely into Cappy, swinging his body to make the animal swerve toward Eddie's horse as he lunged. Eddie fired instantly; but the target was moving, and Jim felt the sting of the bullet along the inside of his arm just as Cappy smashed into the other horse.

Eddie's horse was knocked off his feet. The big sorrel Jim was riding stumbled badly as he hurtled over the other animal, but Jim spurred him again, raking his sides ruthlessly. With a wild snort, Cappy plunged up and away, running with his head thrown to one side to avoid the trailing reins.

Jim bent low over his shoulder, hearing the furious shouts and the blaze of gunfire that broke out behind him. Then Cappy shot into the trees, running wild and dodging like a jack rabbit while Jim kept a sharp lookout for low-hanging limbs that could brain him.

The timber held, thick and scraggly, for half a mile before the country broke into a chaos of brush-choked canyons. As Cappy fled along the rim of one of them, Jim flashed a look over his shoulder to be sure the other riders were not yet in sight. Then he rammed the spurs hard into the sorrel and threw himself out of the saddle.

He fell sheer for fifteen feet, landing in thick brush that gave under his weight, breaking his fall before letting go of him and flipping back into place. He caromed off a rock that would have caved in his chest if his headlong plunge had not been slowed. Then he came up hard against the trunk of a stunted oak and, bruised and breathless, dragged his body fully under its shelter.

He rolled over to look up toward the rim of the canyon and could see nothing except a tangle of brush. A wild hope rose in him. If Cappy kept running, it would take time for the men to trail him down; and time would be working for Jim.

He wanted time to kill Grant Talbot. Jim had never forgotten his dad's words, that Grant had to be stopped for the good of everyone; but he had never thought of Marilyn as being one of those to benefit by Grant's death. This last treachery of Grant's showed clearly that Marilyn was included. Marilyn most of all. The man who killed Grant would be doing her a service, even though she hated him for it; and, given any kind of break, that man was going to be Jim Dixon.

He lay unmoving as he heard the hard pound of running horses. They were on Cappy's track and were following it, apparently, with little difficulty. They thundered past above him without pause, and for a moment Jim lay still, feeling the ease of a terrible tension. Then he struggled out from under the oak and started looking for a rock sharp enough to cut his bonds.

He had just found one, a jagged outcropping in the wall of the canyon, when he heard the horses coming back. Jim dove flat into the brush, his heart hammering. It would be bitterly ironic if this wild gamble netted him nothing but torture, after all. The horses were trotting, and he could hear a harsh, railing voice lifted above the clatter of their hoofs. Then he heard another horse approaching at a walk from upcountry, startling him. He hadn't been able to tell how many horses went by before, but he knew now that either Eddie or his horse had been hurt in that fall.

Jim froze as the men met directly above him; and Eddie's voice came to him, tight with pain.

"Where'd you pick up his horse?"

"Down here about a mile," Slim answered. "Looked like he'd fallen down, but Jim wasn't on him when he did it. That son-of-a-buck quit him along here somewhere."

Eddie's only answer was a string of savage curses that brought a cold sweat out on Jim.

"If Tommy hadn't been so damned clumsy," Slim went on angrily, "I'd have got a clear shot at him when he was first startin' out. What was the idea, bumpin' your horse into me that way?"

"My horse spooked," Tommy snapped back. "Hell, I was tryin' to get a shot at him, too!"

"What the hell did you hear?" Eddie demanded.

"I thought I heard a horse comin'."

"Aw, it's just your damned imagination," Slim said hotly. "You been jumpier'n a woman ever since you got a look at that Miller girl."

"Well, he won't get far," Eddie said grimly, "afoot and with his hands tied. We'll go pick up Grant and then trail him down. And, by God, I'll strip him and use a skinnnin' knife, myself!"

Jim did not move until the sound of the horses had died out completely. Then, cautiously, he wormed out from under the brush and struggled to his feet. The recent activity had restored some of the circulation in his arms and they were burning with the fires of hell; but he put his back to the rock and forced his wrists up and down over the jagged edge of it. It was clumsy as well as painful, and the rope was slippery with his blood before he felt the strands sagging apart.

With his arms free, Jim clawed his way out of the brush and turned onto the tracks of the four horses, bound for Hell's Canyon. He was aware of a fatigue that made his legs heavy and made each step a dragging effort. His hands were swollen, stiff, and useless; but he pounded them together and swung his arms to restore life to them. He didn't have a weapon of any kind but he would get one, some way. His hatred and his driving desire for vengeance would no longer be denied.

As he came out on the last steep slope, he paused, looking down into the snarl of brush, timber, and rocks that made up Hell's Canyon. He had been in the canyon once before, when he was a kid, and he remembered the old prospector's cabin, long deserted, that stood near a deep, never failing spring. The men he was following had rimmed out less than half a mile above the old cabin, and the tracks of their horses angled down into the brush toward it. It was the logical place for them to meet Grant.

Jim turned off the tracks and headed as straight as the jumbled country would permit toward the shack, moving through the brush with the quick stealth of an Indian. His hands had quit their tingling and he flexed his fingers constantly as he advanced, feeling the strength come back into them. He made no plans beyond reaching the cabin. After that, his actions would depend entirely on the breaks that fell to him.

He reached the small clearing in which the cabin stood and stopped, seeing the saddled horses standing before the open door and seeing, with a savage leap of his blood, the Ladder horse among them. Grant had arrived. A small wisp of smoke drifted out of a vacant window at the back of the log shack. Evidently the men had built a small fire inside, on the dirt floor, for the preparation of a hurried meal.

Then he saw Slim sitting on a rock at the edge of the clearing not over twenty-five feet away, whittling with long, disgusted strokes. Apparently he had been left on guard, but his attitude showed plainly that he still thought the strange horse only a figment of Tommy's imagination.

Jim's breath tightened. He glanced once at the gun riding low on Slim's right side, glanced once at the glinting steel of the knife in his hand. Then swiftly and silently he withdrew into heavier brush and circled to come in behind the cowboy. He was going to have that gun.

Just short of his goal, Jim paused for a quick survey of the cabin, hearing the low run of voices but seeing no one. Then he slid out of the brush and stepped toward the rock.

At the last moment Slim sensed his presence and whirled to his feet, his recognition of peril simultaneous with his reaction. Without a second's hesitation, he lunged straight at Jim, the wicked, long-bladed jackknife lifting for a deadly thrust. Jim leaped at the time, dodging and grabbing Slim's wrist in both hands to shove the knife aside. Then he let go with his left hand, flashing his arm around Slim's shoulders and twisting to throw him, bending the cowboy's right arm in toward his body as they fell.

They slammed to the ground with terrific force, Jim on top. As they lit, he heard Slim catch his breath, a strangled gasp, and the cowboy's body jerked convulsively. For a second he held rigid while Jim kept his grip, wondering where the knife had caught him. Then, with a long, shuddering sigh, Slim went limp and unresisting in Jim's grasp.

Jim abruptly stood up, flashing a swift glance at the cabin that reassured him. Then he pulled Slim over on his back. The knife, caught under his weight, had driven to the handle into his chest. The man was dead. Without pause, Jim pulled the gun from his holster, checked it, then leaned to get a sixth cartridge from the cowboy's belt. With the gun fully loaded, Jim turned with long, tight strides toward the cabin, wondering just where Tommy stood in this. If he stood on the wrong side, Jim's troubles would soon be over. Eddie and Grant he might be able to handle, with the element of surprise on his side. Three men he could not take.

Perhaps Tommy really had thought he heard a horse. Perhaps his own horse really had spooked when he spoiled Slim's aim. Or perhaps Jim's friendship and thought of Donna Miller had wrought a change in the cowboy, had taken away his appetite for murder. It was a question hammering at Jim's brain, but it did not slow his relentless strides.

As he circled the group of horses to approach the door of the cabin, he heard Grant offer someone a drink.

"No," Eddie said flatly, "and you better lay off, too. This job isn't finished yet."

"We've got him," Grant said with smug satisfaction. "He can't get away from us, and I'm celebratin'."

"Hop to it," Eddie said shortly.

As Jim stepped into the doorway, he saw it all in one flashing glance. The saddlebags lying in the middle of the floor, in which Grant had evidently brought their meager supplies. The fire just under the window in the far corner, in which sat a rusty tin can with boiling coffee. Tommy knelt before the fire, mixing bread in a small flour sack. Eddie stood behind him and to his left, his right arm folded across his body as if to bolster a broken rib. Grant, his big body supported on wide-braced legs, stood to the right of the fire, and he was in the act of tipping a pint bottle.

As Jim's shadow darkened the doorway, Eddie glanced over his shoulder and then spun, drawing both guns with incredible speed. Jim shot him as he came around. The slug took him in the side, slamming him back against the wall; but he sustained the shock and fired his right-hand gun at the same time Jim fired again. Both bullets took effect.

Eddie dropped his left-hand gun and grabbed at the wall to brace himself as the slug tore into his chest. Jim felt the shock, but he didn't know where he was hit until his left leg gave way under him, letting him down. As he was falling, he saw Tommy spring erect beside the fire, whirl for one swift, horrified glance, then dive headfirst out the window. He saw Grant jerk the bottle away from his lips, staring for a split second in stupefaction before flinging the bottle away from him and reaching desperately for his gun.

Jim was aware of all that; but he kept his eyes on Eddie, who was clinging to life with a vicious tenacity. His eyes gleamed in his gray face, his lips curling back over his teeth in a hideous snarl as he strove to lift his gun. Jim caught his weight on his left hand, hearing the crash of Grant's first shot as he drove a third bullet into Eddie's straining body.

It took him through the middle, smashing the stiffness out of him. His head fell back against the wall and his gun sagged. Even as Jim turned his gun on Grant, he saw Eddie falling toward the fire, heard the hoarse, bubbling cry that was torn out of his throat as he tried to shove himself off it.

Then Jim was looking up into the scarred face of Grant Talbot. In the fleeting seconds since Eddie had first spotted Jim, Grant had got off only one shot. He fired again just as Jim turned, shoving the gun out in front of him with a sharp, violent eagerness. The bullet plowed into the floor scant inches from Jim's stomach, and he fired swiftly up at Grant, seeing the bullet take the big man high in the left shoulder. It seemed to have no effect on him at all. Grant fired again, and the slug hit Jim's extended gun, tearing it out of his hand and sending it spinning beyond reach.

Grant yelled, a harsh, incoherent cry, as he saw his enemy down and weaponless. Jim saw the wild light of triumph that sprang into his eyes while he hung poised, his gun lifted out of line for a gloating second. As the gun started down, Jim grabbed the saddlebags off the floor and flung them straight into Grant's face. Grant threw up his left arm instinctively, his shot going wild as he ducked back.

With a violent lurch, Jim shoved up on his good leg and dove at Grant. He got his arms around the man, drove him back against the wall, then hung on stubbornly, as his wounded leg dragged him down.

Grant fell on top of him, a solid weight that drove the air out of his lungs and set up shooting lights before his eyes; but he twisted, using his good leg for leverage, and flung Grant over on his back. He couldn't hold him there. Grant broke his grip and threw him off, rolling to get at him again. Jim saw that Grant had lost his gun in the fall, and a savage exultation poured through him.

He jammed his knee into Grant's stomach as the man fell on him, hearing the explosive grunt the blow forced through Grant's lips, feeling the blood from Grant's shoulder splashing into his face. He knocked aside the hands that were groping for his throat and grabbed Grant around the neck and shoulder, heaving him to the side and rolling with him to pin him down. The acrid smoke from burning cloth and flesh got into his throat and choked him, and for a moment he lay heavy on Grant, fighting to hold him down.

He couldn't do it. Grant twisted him over, then jackknifed to drive his legs into Jim and kick him away One of those heavy boots dug into the wound in his thigh, and Jim felt sickness well up in him as he landed flat on his back. For a moment he couldn't move. He watched as Grant got to his knees, then made for his gun.

Jim forced his body over, trying to struggle to his hands and knees; but his left leg was a dead weight and he couldn't make it. He could see the guns Eddie had dropped, only a few feet away. As Grant twisted back, his gun lifting, Jim got his good leg under him and threw himself headlong toward those guns. He lit flat on his stomach, hearing the crash of Grant's gun as he strained for one of Eddie's. His hand closed over it and he rolled onto his back, tilting the gun up over his body and waiting a split second for his sight to clear.

Grant was on his knees against the wall, his gun shoved far out in front of him as he triggered frantically. Jim felt the hot breath of a bullet past his cheek. Then Eddie's gun was bucking in his hand, and he saw the dust puff out of Grant's shirt as the bullets, one after another, plowed into his big body.

Jim emptied the gun, firing the last shot as Grant jerked to his feet. It was a convulsive movement that brought him nearly erect before he fell back against the wall and hung there for a moment, bracing himself on rigid legs. His glittering eyes were still fastened on Jim, but they were changing, widening with shocked realization. The gun slipped out of his fingers. Then, slowly, he slid down the wall and rolled loosely on the floor.

Jim let go of the gun in his hand, feeling the solid weight of it on his stomach as he closed his eyes and tried to fight down the sickness that was in him. He was aware, vaguely, that someone cut the cloth away from his wounded leg and started bandaging it. Then he saw Tommy, his face ghastly, working over him.

"Is it bad?" Jim whispered.

Tommy jumped at the sound of his voice. "It ain't broke," he said shakily, "but it's sure bleedin'."

"Tie it tight."

Tommy ducked his head to wipe his sweating chin on his shoulder, without pausing in the swift job his hands were doing. Jim watched the boy dully, knowing that Tommy hadn't dived through that window because of cowardice. It was because he couldn't turn his gun against Jim and wouldn't turn it against men who trusted him. He knew, too, that Tommy had been acting deliberately when he gave him the break he needed.

Jim didn't voice his thoughts, closing his eyes and feeling the numbness of complete exhaustion settle over him. Tommy finished bandaging the leg, then went outside, returning presently with an armload of saddle blankets. He dragged Grant's body over to the corner where Eddie lay sprawled face down over the ashes of the fire he had smothered. He threw a couple of the blankets over them, then made a bed for Jim near the door and helped him onto it. He brought in a saddle to use for a pillow and

193

also fetched a can of clear spring water. Then he hunkered on his spurs beside Jim and looked at him squarely, a look of shame on his face.

"I've hobbled the horses," he said slowly, "all except mine. I'll head straight over the mountain and should be back sometime tonight with the doctor. I'll bring a camp outfit, too. You may be here for several days."

"All right."

"I'll bring Skeet Dorman, too, and I'll tell him the truth about this whole rotten mess." Tommy hesitated, then said bitterly, "He'll be glad to know it was Slim and Eddie and me that's been doin' this rustlin'."

"Goin' to turn yourself in, are you?"

"Yeah, I—" Tommy broke off, shaking his head and swallowing hard. "I was gettin' pretty near happy until Eddie come up with this deal."

It was all Jim needed to know. "Skeet Dorman," he said, forcing his weak, husky voice, "is a mighty reasonable man. He's made a mistake or two himself and knows how easy it is to do. When you get through tellin' him about the rustlin' you've done, tell him you're still on the Five Drag payroll and I'd like to keep you there."

Tommy caught his breath, his eyes widening with incredulity.

"And I was goin' to tell you," Jim finished, "that as far as I know, the trail to Donna is wide open."

"She'd never have a rustler!"

"No, but if she knew she'd changed a fella from a rustler into a man—"

Jim left the sentence hanging, watching Tommy and seeing the fire of hope springing to life in him. Then he closed his eyes and didn't look up as he heard Tommy hurry from the cabin and gallop away.

As the sound of the horse faded out, Jim became aware of a barren loneliness such as he had never known. The fight was over. But the knowledge of that brought only a dull satisfaction.

He knew the valley would have peace now and, ultimately, prosperity. The range was coming back strongly since the summer rains, and cattle were picking up. He knew there would be rustling and outlawry in this far-flung land for a long time to come, but never again on such a devastating scale. The country would grow up. It would be safe for women and kids. And there would be Five Drag cows in it, as Long John Dixon had hoped.

The old ranch was secure. Jim would be free to repair the house, rebuild the bunkhouse and barn, set up a fitting headquarters for the vast spread he had envisioned. But he found that he could not visualize it as home without Marilyn. She would never believe the story Tommy had to tell, and even if she did—

Weakness and exhaustion gradually blotted out Jim's dreary thoughts, putting him to sleep in spite of his pain. The touch of a cool hand on his face awakened him, and he looked up to see Marilyn kneeling over him, her eyes brimming with tears she couldn't hold back. Behind her, Jim saw Skeet, looking down with grim, clouded eyes.

It was a jarring note. That he should see Marilyn in the wildness of delirium seemed natural enough, but Skeet Dorman had no place in his dreams. Then he felt the splash of a very real tear on his cheek, and he blinked.

"Oh, Jim! Are you all right?" Marilyn cried anxiously.

"All right?" he echoed, staring at her blankly, still doubting his senses.

She clutched his shoulder. "Jim, tell me what happened. Where is everybody? Who shot you?"

Her frantic words jolted Jim wide awake. He saw then that she was terribly agitated, on the verge of collapse; but she hadn't looked around the cabin. She didn't know—

Jim suddenly didn't have air enough in his lungs. He tried to drag in more and couldn't and finally whispered, "Eddie shot me."

'Oh, Jim, I knew what he was planning, but I couldn't—Listen." Her hurried, stammering voice was low, broken by a tightness in her throat. "That night after you were at the ranch I couldn't sleep. I took a walk, saw Eddie ride in. I heard him talking to Grant. Jim, it was terrible! They argued a little before they—made their deal. Eddie threw it up to Grant about killing your dad, lying about Elliott, hanging Uncle Dave. Grant—finally admitted."

She had to stop, shaking her head fiercely and fighting for self-control. Jim looked wildly up at Dorman, torn between hope and doubt. The old lawman had his hand on Marilyn's shoulder, his deeply lined face as grave as Jim had ever seen it.

"I was paralyzed," Marilyn went on, struggling to hold her voice level. "After Eddie left, Grant came out to the hall and saw me standing there. He knew I'd heard. His eyes! He grabbed me, locked me up. I couldn't get away till after he left, late last night. Jim, all those hours! Knowing what they were going to do, helpless, tortured by the mean things I'd said to you! Then last night, trying to catch up with you, fearing to find you dead—I couldn't stand it! But thank God we got here in time. Where is Eddie now? Did he go to meet Grant?"

Jim glanced helplessly up at Skeet, then looked away and said hoarsely, "The fight's over, Marilyn."

"Over? What do you mean?"

"Grant—already got here."

Jim looked back at her, wanting to say more. He couldn't. Marilyn seemed to have stopped breathing, fixing him with a blank, frozen stare. Skeet glanced swiftly around the cabin, then abruptly stood up to stride to the blanket-covered figures in the corner. Marilyn started to turn, to look after him; but Jim grabbed her wrist, pulling her back and holding her with a hard, commanding gaze.

Dorman came back and said huskily, "A hard job to do, Jim, but it had to be done." Then, hurriedly, he left the cabin.

A moment longer Marilyn stared at Jim, her eyes widening with comprehension. Then she dropped her face into her hands and let herself go, sobbing uncontrollably. Jim lay rigid, staring at the ceiling, feeling those sobs go through him like knives. He knew that twenty-two years of loving a brother couldn't be wiped out in a moment, even by disillusion. It seemed an eternity to him before the sobs eased and finally ceased, and Marilyn lifted a white, tragic face.

"He was always good to me, Jim. I can't hate him—even knowing—"

"He was wild, Marilyn," Jim said, with quick earnestness. "We've all been wild. But most of that wild blood has been spilled now, includin' mine. There are better days comin' if you—if we—"

He stammered to a halt, aware of the little hand that was stealing into his. He clamped down on it, tight, reaching his other hand for her shoulder as she started to bend over him. He could see the shadow of grief lifting from her eyes, could see a light coming through that was familiar yet deeper, stronger than when he had seen it last, four years ago.

"Can you ever forgive me?" she whispered. "Ever love me again?"

"Love you!" he breathed, and pulled her to him.

THE END

www.ingramcontent.com/pod-product-compliance
Lightning Source LLC
Chambersburg PA
CBHW030158200626
46812CB00017B/2628